In Praise of *Shine Your Light*
By J.R. Matheson &
Lee Bice-Matheson

Shine Your Light is a delightful and insightful novel, one that sheds light on all that it surveys. It beautifully describes the incredible adventures of the youthful Paige Maddison (familiar from the authors' previous and popular novels) who while still a high-school student is wise beyond her years. As well, she is an intuitive person whose feet are firmly planted on the ground, though at times she seems to have her head in the clouds, where she communes with the spirits of Archangels Raphael and Michael, King Solomon, Grey Owl, and even the dreaded Beelzebub! Like many of her high-school girlfriends, Paige is a well-rounded and purposeful personality, so much so that I found myself thinking about her as the Nancy Drew of the realm of high spirits and dreams and visions, traumatic experiences and out-of-body trips, all convincingly described! She almost single-handedly sets the world aright. Readers who enjoy learning about "medicine bundles" and "earth religions," as well as being carried along by descriptions of lively human beings with whom it is easy to identify, will find this well-wrought work of fantasy to their liking. In my opinion, it is "a keeper." It is also (risking a pun) a Paige-turner.

—*John Robert Colombo, Author and Anthologist*

Shine Your Light is a unique blend of Biblical quest and supernatural adventure, as Paige Maddison experiences her spiritual awakening and joins forces with angels and shape-shifters to fight the most important battle of her life. A very enjoyable and deeply spiritual addition to the Paige Maddison series.

—*Philip Henry, Author and Film-maker*

In Praise of *Shine Your Light*

Shine Your Light, the third instalment of the *Paige Maddison Series* is a heart stopper. The ongoing struggle between good and evil plays itself out on the O'Brien Estate with ever increasing intensity. The protagonist is Paige, a seventeen-year-old young woman, who has spiritual powers and helpers revealed through a crescendo of events. The antagonist is the mysterious Ariana desperate to locate the ancient Seal of Solomon and its accompanying grimoire. Helped by black magic and the prima-demon Beelzebul the struggle ends in an epic battle between Paige and Ariana. The epilogue provides a lesson in life sure to be beneficial to all young adults. I enjoyed it thoroughly.

—*David D. Plain, Award Winning Author*

In *Shine Your Light*, authors Lee Bice-Matheson and J.R. Matheson pose the question: what would happen if one does not fulfill their destiny and allows darkness to prevail? This novel is electrifying, fast-paced and full of genuine emotion as it transcends matters such as self-doubt and evil. The authors explore and expose details from various sources allowing the reader to learn and grow alongside the heroine. We meet new characters who are gratifyingly developed, namely the villain who aided the plot in becoming the most thrilling and inspiring novel of the trilogy. Paige is transformed throughout her explorations and conquers all with the help of her gifts, angels, respected mentors, family and friends. The authors leave us with a final notion that we must trust our own instincts and ultimately come from a place of love.

—*Katy Slana, Beta Reader*

For Vivian°
Enjoy Paige's Journey
LuAnn xo

SHINE YOUR LIGHT

LuAnn Mattson & JR

CAROL'S LOG CABIN

GRANDFATHER ROCK

GRANDFATHER ROCK

EMERALD LAKE

PEGGY'S COTTAGE

PAIGE MADDISON SERIES

C. SLIPACOFF

SHINE YOUR LIGHT

BRAD'S HOUSE

COTTAGE

NATURAL ARCHWAY

GUEST HOUSE

CEMETERY

O'BRIEN MANOR

PAIGE MADDISON SERIES

SHINE YOUR LIGHT

C. SLIPACOFF

SHINE YOUR LIGHT

PAIGE MADDISON SERIES
Book Three

LEE BICE-MATHESON
& J.R. MATHESON

Suite 300 - 990 Fort St
Victoria, BC, V8V 3K2
Canada

www.friesenpress.com

ISBN
978-1-4602-9995-1 (Hardcover)
978-1-4602-9996-8 (Paperback)
978-1-4602-9997-5 (eBook)

1. YOUNG ADULT FICTION

Distributed to the trade by The Ingram Book Company

J.R. and I dedicate this book to all of the unsung
heroes who tirelessly help others, unnoticed.

***

Quote Investigator: This remark apparently was made by
Einstein during an interview that was published in *The
Saturday Evening Post* in 1929. Here is an excerpt showing the
context of his comment. The first paragraph below records
Einstein's words; the next sentence is the interviewer speak-
ing; the final paragraph is Einstein speaking again:

*"I believe in intuitions and inspirations. I sometimes feel that
I am right. I do not know that I am. When two expeditions of
scientists, financed by the Royal Academy, went forth to test my
theory of relativity, I was convinced that their conclusions would
tally with my hypothesis. I was not surprised when the eclipse of
May 29, 1919, confirmed my intuitions. I would have been surprised if I had been wrong."*

*"Then you trust more to your imagination than to your
knowledge?"*

*"I am enough of the artist to draw freely upon my imagination.
Imagination is more important than knowledge. Knowledge is
limited. Imagination encircles the world."*

http://quoteinvestigator.com/2013/01/01/einstein-imagi-
nation/ Garson O'Toole

CHAPTER ONE

Snowflakes danced and swirled beyond the windowpane, capturing the sun's rays, glistening like diamonds as they drifted,
mesmerizing me as I stood by and watched without a care in
the world. Mother Nature had trapped me tight within her
grasp. I was drawn into her beauty and magnetic, overpowering energy. Snowflakes accumulated, forming small mounds
and snow drifts, and I viewed the scene as if through the lens
of time-lapse photography. I sensed danger was near, yet felt
warm and peaceful inside. And then I sensed nothing at all.

***

My instincts snapped me into a state of high alert as I
searched carefully inside a dimly lit room, arms outstretched,
hoping I wouldn't bump into something and wound myself.
I blinked my eyes repeatedly and as my vision returned,
images penetrated my consciousness. Eyesight sharpened,
I spied a shimmering, oval, mahogany table with twelve
handsomely crafted wooden chairs with etched frames
and deep-cushioned red-velvet seats. The table caught the
sunlight peeking in from beyond the dining room, through

the kitchen window with its tiny panes of glass and lattice framing. It was of a time long ago.

I approached the back door and peeked out through a tall, narrow side window. I gasped as I spied a dense forest filled with 100-year-old pine, birch, oak, and black walnut trees all coexisting as one, their branches intertwined. Something seemed familiar about this place. I found my courage and it urged me to continue exploring my new surroundings. I passed through a low-set hallway and noticed two bedrooms across from one another. Each room contained twin beds, and I assumed the children's room was the one with colourful quilts adorned with patches of birds and animals. There were carvings in that particular room which drew me in. One carving was of a beaver, another was of a moose, and the third a wolf's head. It was much larger than the others, and it captured my attention, as the wolf was a kindred spirit to me. I ran my fingers along its nose and felt the etching on its face, wondering who had created this beautiful work of art.

***

An energy burst punched me in the gut, and I awoke seated in a high-back wing chair facing a wall of leather-bound books, placed neatly in alphabetical order on a floor-to-ceiling bookcase. My eyes played tricks on me, as the illuminating light diminished as if on a timed dimmer switch. I approached the front window and pressed my face against the pane. Snow covered every inch of the window, and I trembled at the realization that I was trapped inside. I zipped up my treasured royal-blue down parka gifted to me from mom and remembered the last thing I had said to my grandparents' caregiver Hanna—*Send help if I'm not back by the end of the day.* How long had it been since I left O'Brien Manor? The crisp smell of freshly laid snowfall seeped into the cottage and froze my nose hairs, engorging my nostrils. As I wiggled my nose, my mind wandered to the fact that, somehow, I had transitioned back in time to the cozy but elegant surroundings of yesteryear.

***

Without a moment's notice, I was yanked back in time as if through a tunnel, caught in a liminal state between two parallel worlds. Relying on my spatial memory this time, I fumbled through the dining room and navigated my way down the hall to explore the master bedroom. Light spilled in through a tiny, round window as I entered, allowing me to study the black-and-white photos set in matchstick frames hung on the load-bearing wall. My eyes widened as I spotted a picture of a family of four. Moving closer to look at them, it sunk in. There stood Conall and his little sister, Mackenzie, holding hands. She had on the white jumper, her long hair tied back with a ribbon and carefully positioned over her right shoulder, and Conall was dressed in his favourite goth clothes—a white ruffled shirt and black skinny pants. The parents stood on either side of the children. Then I noticed something—the mom was the angel from the cemetery. Sasha Grace, their mother, was in the photo in human form. She was beautiful, with long braided hair falling on each shoulder and a plain but shapely dress with fabric eyelets on the waistband. The father must have been Lyle "Mac" McDonough, who had been indebted to my family, the O'Briens. I could see the black cloud he nurtured reflected on his stern, brooding face, eyes narrowed. Seeing Conall's family like this made me shiver. I had only known three of the family members in their spirit forms; I wondered if I would be meeting Mac sometime soon. A cold breeze washed over me and I shuddered.

A slight ringing in my ears distracted me, and I caught sight of a tiny tin bell that sat on the nightstand next to the double bed. I noticed the back of a man's head with short, tousled black hair and assumed it must be Mac lying there. He was wrapped tightly within the bedding. Sasha Grace strode past me carrying a tray laden with some sort of medicine bottle and tea cup and saucer. She eased the tray onto the nightstand. Poor Mac coughed and choked as he struggled to sit up. Glancing towards the doorway, I recognized their two children, Conall and Mackenzie, clutching each other's hand. It was surreal to see them in the flesh. They watched from the shadows, a look of anguish sprawled across their faces, and then they shut their eyes tight to fight the tears. A shriek erupted from Sasha Grace. I turned in time to see Mac expel a long breath and collapse over the side of the bed, catching the tray as he went. The crashing sound pierced my eardrums, and then I heard his head hit the wooden floorboards with a thud. There was no more movement from him. I realized I was a witness to the last few minutes of their father's life. Tears welled up in my eyes as I watched Sasha Grace throw herself on top of her husband, crying out his name. Conall and Mackenzie flopped on top of their mom. I recalled Conall's story of his father's death from the day he terrorized Bradley Adam Parkman and me in the basement of O'Brien Manor, and I knew this was the saddest moment for the McDonough family, the catalyst for their family's breakdown. Watching their father die shook my world. As heart-wrenching as the scene was, I could not help but think of my dad and dreaded the day death would visit our doorstep.

Panicked, I ran from the bedroom and barely remembered entering the McDonough's library. I stopped abruptly to admire its beauty, the wall of leather-bound books capturing my attention. First editions, I assumed. Then it occurred to me: this was the same library that gave me the answers to two hauntings on the O'Brien estate — one by Conall, who accused my family of his father's demise, and the second by Bradford and the tortured young boy; Grandpa channeled an Edgar Allan Poe poem with clues to that haunting. Somehow, the library seemed grander now. An English leather chair and mahogany side table were positioned next to the wing chair I'd awakened in earlier, and they faced the wall of books. On the table sat an ugly tortoiseshell ram's head with a chain attached to a tiny spoon and brush. As I pondered the significance of the ram's head, I saw a flash, followed by the image of a gentleman snorting black powder from his thumb and index finger and the words *snuff mull* spelled as if on a ticker tape. I guessed it was tobacco. Trying to ignore this vision, I closed my eyes and pictured the old dilapidated cottage's weathered library as I had first discovered it weeks after our move to Camlachie. It overwhelmed me to think that somehow I stood in the same place with my footing in two very different centuries. More importantly, I realized perhaps I was trapped indefinitely between parallel worlds: present day — snowbound in the cottage and living with my grandparents on the O'Brien estate — and a century ago, observing the McDonough family. I slumped into the leather chair, feeling helpless.

***

Imagine having an out-of-body experience, floating up towards heaven, pushing past white, fluffy clouds in an azure-blue sky and into the darkness of the universe, with stars shining brightly as guiding lights. Like turning light bulbs on, one by one, each star led the way until ... I was in the midst of a rectangular room. Blended with the white light was an outline of a man in a floor-length gown, standing tall with outstretched arms, His hands hidden by cuffs. He had long white hair and blazing blue eyes, and He was a beautiful sight to behold. I sat in a wooden chair as He pointed his long, skinny index finger to my left. The vision of the young boy being tortured in the O'Brien manor's ice vault room was playing as if on a movie theatre screen. This time I saw his punisher. He had a slight build, bald head, and the craziest eyes, and he brutalized the boy with a 3-lash whip. I could not understand why I had to see this again and stared back at the man in white. He looked sternly at me and pointed His finger dramatically so I would once again witness the abuse. Forced to observe the boy, I heard words bellowed by the man.

"Leave his body, demon. You cannot have my son any longer. He is a good soul, and you cannot have him. I call upon God, Archangel Michael, and Archangel Raphael for help to expel this demon!" The man drew the sign of a cross on his chest.

I skipped a breath as I realized this man was not the boy's abuser but his father trying to save his son from ... a demon! Grasping my pounding chest, I caught sight of the angels. Archangel Michael's energy was strong, heightened by his magnificent presence. He had broad shoulders and was clothed from head to toe in a beige-and-white tie-dyed robe, his voluminous white wings outstretched at his sides. His long, flowing blond hair and baby-blue eyes hypnotized me. I remembered him from the day he taught me how to heal Allan at the guesthouse. I assumed his companion was Archangel Raphael. He knelt next to the boy and had a quiet, yet powerful, disposition. He had fine, light-brown hair that fell to his jawline, and he was of medium build, wearing a belted, beige robe. His white, outstretched wings were wider and more streamlined than Archangel Michael's. The saviours planted their hands on the boy's head and heart.

A black, wispy soul drifted up from the boy's body as he fell limp. Archangel Michael seized the essence of the soul and vanished. Archangel Raphael remained behind, stooped over the boy's body. He recited prayers in a language I didn't know and then, *poof*, he disappeared. The boy showed signs of life and inhaled a deep breath. His father picked him up and cried for joy.

Snapping out of the vision, I was happy to see the boy had been saved by his father and survived the ordeal. I also celebrated knowing that our family had not been responsible for his beating. Then I wondered why the haunting by Bradford had occurred on Halloween and why he had threatened my family and accused them of a past cruelty. My ancestors, the O'Briens, were wrongfully accused of this tragedy by the boy's uncle named Bradford. Perhaps, sometimes, spirits could be inaccurate in their memory when charged with anger. Perhaps they lashed out at those living near to their last memory tied to a room in a haunted manor.

Emotionally drained from the vision, I fell into a deep sleep. I dreamt that I was back in the same room again with the man in the white robe. This time, still seated in the chair, He pointed His finger to my right.

***

An overpowering sense of relief washed over me as I watched my friends burst into the cottage. Allan Brewer sported a full-grown black beard and mustache contrasting his long Elvis like sideburns, piercing sage, blue eyes, and well-toned physique. His stepdaughter, Trixie, followed on his heels, her long, black hair flowing and wearing a sad, pale face. My BFF, Carole, forcefully entered the room, her shoulder-length black hair tossed back revealing her soulful dark-brown eyes. Tears streamed down her tanned face. Visually, they all looked the same–furrowed brows, concerned looks, and the realization that I was in danger reflected in their dilated pupils. My body lay limp and helpless on the leather chair, and I was forced to observe the scene from afar as I hovered above them. Note to self: *I don't think I'll ever become accustomed to an out-of-body experience. Yet, it was fascinating to watch my friends, almost as if caught up in a science experiment. What would they do for me now?* I was relieved and overjoyed with their arrival. As if in slow motion, Allan approached my body and tried to revive me with mouth-to-mouth resuscitation. I felt I was past the point of saving. *Perhaps I am dead.*

I wanted to shout from the roof tops, "I'm alive!" In fact, I tried to yell it from my floating vantage point near the ceiling, but no one heard me. The amusement ended. I searched the room for signs of spirit energy and there were none. My grandfather once reminisced about our Celtic roots, that some folks who had a near-death experience recounted seeing a white light or a relative to help bring them home. I saw neither. And then I heard a voice asking me a question in a matter-of-fact tone.

Do you want to leave now?

I knew, deep in my soul, this question had a life-or-death response.

No, I am not ready to go, I pleaded. *I have my parents, grandparents, as well as my friends to protect. They need me. Not yet, please ... I beg you.*

***

I awoke in my body with a shudder. Squeals of delight filled the room, and all three of my friends rushed to hug me. I raised my arm part way as a warning. My rescuers stopped dead in their tracks.

"Paige, you're okay! You've been missing for three days. With the snowfall ... we couldn't get to you. The cemetery and its surroundings are piled high. We had to wait until we could climb the ridge. Oh my goodness. You do have a guardian angel looking after you," exclaimed Carole, tears of joy flowing down her cheeks.

"Carole, give Paige a moment. She just woke up," Allan said. He knelt beside me and carefully wiped the curls from my face. My heart skipped a beat.

Trixie peeked around her stepfather's shoulder and peered at me. "Paige, we're so thankful you're okay. I don't know what my daddy and I ..." Trixie's shoulders shook, and I knew she was crying.

I pushed back into the leather chair and looked into my friends' eyes as I said, "Thank ... you. Water?"

Trixie opened a bottle and poured it carefully over my lips. I gulped it down as some of it spilled onto my chest. I had never experienced a thirst like that before.

"Thanks ... Trixie." I gave her a half smile as I studied her. She looked like a china doll with her pale face, and hypnotic, red-flecked, brown eyes. For a brief moment, I had a flashback to the last time I saw her here, in the cottage, lying listlessly on the floor. "Trixie, are you healed?" I asked.

"I am. I had a terrible battle with a wolf from my former pack. It's not important now. I'll explain it later, Paige. Thanks for asking."

Dizziness mixed with a bit of nausea caused me to wince. It crossed my mind that the next time I went into the woods alone, I should definitely call a friend to join me. *How could I put myself in so much danger? And what summoned me to return to the cottage at this time of year?* The answers escaped me. The synapses in my brain were not as active as I knew they should be.

"How are we going to help Paige back to the manor, Allan?" asked Carole.

"I'll carry her over my shoulder if I have to." Allan stared into my eyes, took my hand, and kissed it softly. "Never, ever, do that again, Paige. Next time, please ask me to come with you. Please."

I looked away in shame. I knew Allan was right. "I promise," I replied in a whisper.

Allan stood, sniffed the air, and cocked his ear, listening to the wind howling outside as it sculpted the cottage. "The snowstorm is not letting up. Lucky for us we set out when we did. The ridge will be too difficult in this weather. Trixie, did you grab the supplies?"

"Yes I did, Dad," she responded, her radiant smile lighting up her child-like face. She grabbed an oversized backpack, and I wondered how in the world she had carried it up and over the ridge by herself. Then I remembered the day she protected me from the massive grey wolf. Trixie might be short, but she was surprisingly strong. That memory led to a flashback of shapeshifting into Journey, my inner spirit wolf. Shaking my head to clear away the cobwebs, I heard the last part of her reply.

"... granola bars, mixed nuts, juice boxes, and Carole brought extra water bottles. We should be good for a few days, if we have to."

"Well done. You are my sweet, sweet daughter. My heart sings when I hear you call me Dad."

As her stepfather spoke, Trixie examined him with eyes like saucers. The two had grown closer since they were reunited last fall. She ran to her dad and hugged him tightly. It was a touching moment in such troubled times.

Carole was quiet. I sent her a telepathic thought.

Are you okay?

She replied in kind. *We're in danger. On our way over here, all of a sudden I felt overheated in this frigid weather. I started to sweat and wanted to throw up. I can't grasp what it is, Paige.*

Being in such a fragile state, I was unable to help Carole, who desperately wanted to figure out our next threat and protect us all. She retreated to the kitchen and sighed as she looked out through the tall, narrow window next to the worn kitchen door. The snow filled the forest floor and scaled the trunks of the ancient trees. The words *lancet window* popped into my head, and I shrugged off this bit of trivia.

"Remember when we were here last, Paige? Hiding in this same cottage on Halloween ... when your long-time family friend, Dexter, stalked us too, and we flew out the front of the cottage, protected by Allan's soldiers?" Carole asked, not waiting for a response. "The wolves were our saviours. Allan, where are they now?" Her voice sounded stone-cold, and she spun around to confront him.

"They're scattered; they're here ... they're there. Why, Carole?" Allan's eyes narrowed.

As she replied, Carole turned and stared out the window again. "There's a war coming. And for this one, we need all the help we can get." Suddenly, Carole fainted. Trixie bolted, catching her before she hit the wood floor. She sat next to Carole and pulled her into her lap.

My arms and legs tingled, and I felt like crawling out of my skin. Carole's voice was riddled with fear. We were more connected than I had realized—physically and psychically.

"Paige, you're white as a ghost. Here, drink some more water." Allan held my head back and slowly poured it down my throat. I was grateful for him, for all of them.

Catching my breath, I finally blurted, "If something's coming, we need to ask for help from our spirit friends. The angels, the spirit wolves ... and there's another group that might be able to help." I stopped abruptly, worried what my friends might think when they found out whom.

"What group, Paige?" Trixie asked, hesitation resounding in her voice.

"I'm not sure if you're ready for this. You guys aren't going to like it," I answered.

"Please, tell us," Allan said. His blue eyes appeared electric-black as they darted back and forth, studying mine, mere inches from my face.

"Hellhounds!" I exclaimed, and fell back into the chair with a thwack.

CHAPTER TWO

When I came to, I was hovering above my friends, watching them as they paced around my body. I felt sorry for them, having to deal with yet another one of my traumatic experiences. My mind raced wildly as I travelled down a long, winding tunnel only to be pulled into the upper reaches of the universe. I found myself seated in the room with the man with outstretched arms and floor-length white robe. He pointed towards my right. I winced and shut my eyes tight, afraid of what I would be shown this time. Eventually, my stubbornness faded. I opened my eyes and peeked in the direction He'd indicated. I gasped as I gazed upon an expanse of manicured lawns punctuated with massive old trees that towered into the cerulean sky amid a sprinkling of billowing, white clouds. Glancing around, I spied an ultramarine stream so still and calm that it reflected the puffy clouds and sky above. Children played on swing sets, and I could hear their exuberant laughter like musical notes falling upon my ears. The vision was one I did not want to end. The brilliant colours were unlike any I had ever seen before. Then my ears began to twitch as I strained to hear bursts of extraordinary singing. My intuition told me it must be coming from what

I believed was the heavenly host—all of the angels as One. Grandma had told me a story once about this very event.

Snapping back to attention, I studied Him and experienced a glowing warmth that surrounded my body like an overpowering, heartfelt, love-filled hug. It moved into my body and became so intense; I almost toppled backwards right out of my chair. Instead, my hands began to shake. Then my arms quivered, slowly elevating until my hands were high above my head. It scared me, as it seemed to be out of my control. Then I heard a stern, compassionate voice.

Do not fret, child. You are being cleansed. After the haunting on the O'Brien estate, it must be completed. Trust in me.

And I did just that. As soon as my body relaxed into the energy vibrating near me, my arms began to shake rhythmically, in unison. I watched as though I was a third party, captivated by the astonishing event unfolding before me. The warmth inside me felt as if a ray of sunshine had moved in, and any bitterness, resentment, or anger I had bottled up dissipated; I experienced pure joy and peace. Tears streamed down my face.

***

"Paige!" Allan snapped at me. "Wake up, wake up! Oh, this is so frustrating. What is she doing? Why is she moaning like that?"

"Dad, wait. She'll come around," Trixie said. "She always does. Just give her a few minutes."

"Yes, listen to your step ... I mean, your daughter. Paige is a fighter, and there's no way she's leaving her grandparents—or us, for that matter," added Carole. "Let's just focus our positive energy on her, together, until she comes to."

I became frustrated as the concerned voices of my friends faded in and out, as though I was tuning into a radio station from far away. I looked towards my guide, and He smiled and reassured me.

There now, child. You are healed. You can return to your friends. Remember I am guiding you on your rightful path, Paige.

***

Bam! There I was, seated in the leather chair, present day, in the dilapidated cottage. Allan wiped tears from my cheeks as I opened my eyes. My friends pressed their faces near mine, and I withdrew from them. I needed time to process what had just happened. *Is it really God who is guiding me, or His right-hand? Where did that thought come from?*

"Okay, everyone, let's give Paige some room," Allan said. He started to pace in front of the wall of books. Carole and Trixie disappeared behind me. I wondered what they were doing, but I had to gather my thoughts. Time crept by until I was ready to speak.

"I'm not sure if I've hit my head or something," I said, "but I believe I travelled back in time to witness the death of Conall and Mackenzie's father, Mac McDonough. I saw Sasha Grace as a person, not as an angel. And my consciousness travelled to somewhere in the universe, in a room with … God. He made me watch the young boy being tortured by his father in order to draw out a demon." I rested my head upon my right arm, exhausted.

"Oh, that's all," replied Allan. "I don't know what to say, Paige." He frowned at me as he paused to let my words sink in. "Clearly, there's something spiritual going on with you, and it's more than any of us can comprehend. You need to speak to Grey Owl. Remember, he guided you before. Maybe he knows what's happening."

Carole and Trixie tiptoed into the room, but in my mind's eye I had seen them approaching minutes beforehand. It was a part of my gift that I counted on, like taking a breath.

"What's going on?" asked Trixie. "Can we help you, Paige?"

"Only if you know what it's like to travel back in time and have a conversation with God," I jested.

"Say what? Never joke about God!" Carole said. "You need help again, Paige. Maybe Grey—"

"That's what I just said! Great minds think alike." Allan grinned as he marked an X on her shoulder and gave her a playful punch.

"What was that for?" Carole asked as she rubbed her arm. "It hurt!"

"Jinx! Got you! You know, when two people say the same thing ... though we missed the mark. Oh, you're too young to know. It's a child's game I picked up along the way." Allan glanced over at me and changed the subject. "We all need to lighten up. How 'bout we have something to eat. What's left in your backpack, Trixie?"

"How about some more granola bars? My fave," she replied.

We each devoured one granola bar for lunch. It wasn't much, but I understood we were trying to ration the food.

"How long before we're rescued?" I asked. Heads bowed, no one replied. The silence in the room was disheartening until Trixie opened up a conversation with her dad.

"Well, now that we have some time together, Dad, can I please ask you something?"

"Of course, honey," Allan replied. "Anything."

"How long did you know about me before you tracked me down?" Trixie's tears pooled in her eyes as she studied her stepfather.

Allan hesitated, but not for long. "Three, maybe four years, but I was handling a situation on the West Coast. Evil is everywhere, Trixie, and that's what I'm here for. To help banish it." His soulful eyes glistened as he looked at her. Then he rested his hand on hers.

"I was devastated when Mom died, and then I met all of you. My heart was broken in half, but I can feel it mending. I'm still so sad that she died. She was taken out by a deranged black wolf that had this humongous, gnarly, skunk-like tail. I'll never forget the look in his eyes after he ripped her throat out. Pure evil. It makes me shudder to think about it. I'll always be grateful for the pack. They ran him off." Trixie's shoulders drooped.

"I sensed there was trouble with you, but please understand; I couldn't leave my pack to come and help you or your mother. It was a decision that was difficult to make, Trixie. I'm so sorry. You were alone for a while?" Allan's pacing quickened.

"Granite took me in when I shapeshifted for the first time as a young pup. Imagine me ... a black lab accepted into the wolf pack. She was the alpha female in the pack. She tried not to favour me, but the other pups resented our relationship, and they took it out on me. I survived, but looking back ... Thankfully, Granite saved me — twice. Once, when an up-and-coming wolf named Trebur almost knocked me off the side of a cliff, Granite was there. She bit my neck, reeling me back in, or I would've plummeted down to the valley below. She forced Trebur from the pack. And somehow, seven years later, in the midst of all of the chaos on the O'Brien estate, he found me here, and that's who I had the nasty battle with, Paige. Luckily, I won the fight and Archangel Michael healed me in this very cottage. It was hard to come back here, but when your safety was at risk, Paige ... well, I wanted to be here for you."

Trixie's eyes filled with tears, and then she continued. "Another time, a friend turned on me. Her name was Kara. We had fun together running wild through the woods and over ridges, and then one day we were head-to-head, teeth bared. I wondered how we got to that point. Again, Granite appeared out of nowhere and bit Kara hard on her throat, tossing her like a rag doll into a prickly bush. Kara never bothered me after that day, but we were never friends again. It broke my heart."

Carole patted Trixie on the back. "Experiencing your first betrayal from a friend is the hardest, Trixie. I'm sorry this happened to you. We're all grateful you're here. Aren't we?" she asked, looking from one of us to the other.

"Of course," I chimed in with Allan. "But wait, I don't understand. You lived with a wolf pack? When did Dexter and Delia take you in? And how?"

"If I may step in, Trixie?" Allan asked. She nodded at him. "First of all, canines come from a long line of wolves. It's not an exception to take Trixie in. Wolves connect to another's soul, so in keeping with that line of thinking, Granite connected to Trixie's soul and treated her as one of the wolf pack. Carry on, Trixie."

"Thanks, Dad. Then one day, Granite led me out of the forest, and when I tried to follow her home, she turned 'round on me, growling. It scared me half to death. I guess I had reached an age that was unacceptable to continue living with wolves. Dexter found me behind their house and the rest is history. Both Dexter and Delia were so good to me." Trixie shrugged and looked away.

Allan added, "Trixie, we're here together now and that's all that matters. The past is the past. Reliving it only gives way to memories we recreate over time; they're illusions. I've learned to live in the present and appreciate the gift of the here and now. The future will take care of itself. This is the only way I can make it on my path in life. I love you, Daughter."

"I love you too ... Dad."

I watched as Allan bent over to hug Trixie. She pulled him close.

Carole interrupted the sentimental moment and added, "True friendship must stand the test of time, Trixie. A pearl of wisdom I've learned from my Uncle Kyle."

Trixie nodded at Carole. "Yes, I imagine so, Carole," she replied as she broke from the embrace.

I studied Carole for a moment, and it flashed into my mind: *We had only known each other for a short time. Was this a forewarning?* The wind howled outside, and I wrapped my arms around myself. The bitter cold began to seep into my bones, and I worried that my friends may have bitten off more than they could chew in order to save me.

CHAPTER THREE

Bang! Bang! I awoke with a start and wondered where the annoying noises were coming from. I was also a bit startled to find myself wrapped within Allan's arms. We were cradled together on the library floor to remain warm. Trixie and Carole slept in the two chairs, and I wondered why I was the only one hearing the disturbing sounds. One more loud *BANG,* and the cottage door burst wide open. There stood four snow-covered men dressed in full winter clothing, hats and all, with a Fire Department label on their sleeves. The man in the lead was tall and overpowering, sporting a huge, red-handled axe. My heart palpitated and I shook Allan awake as I announced, "Trixie! Carole! We're saved!"

Allan shot upright, and my two girlfriends yawned lazily and looked disinterested until they realized our heroes had arrived.

"Are you guys okay? Which one of you is Paige Maddison?" asked the fireman with the axe. His authoritarian voice caused me to lose mine.

"Uhh ... she's here with me," replied Allan. He grabbed my hand for support.

"Did my ... I mean, did Hanna send you?" I asked, wide-eyed and feeling vulnerable.

"No, actually, it was a neighbour. An older woman named Peggy. Man, that lady has been calling the station since you went missing. She's a stubborn old woman."

I smiled. "Oh, don't we know it. But thank you for telling us."

"Normally the paramedics are first responders, but with the snowstorms and all, we were ordered to intervene by our captain — Captain George. We don't have much time, either. Another storm is on its way."

Carole added telepathically, *I knew she'd come through for us, Paige. Peggy loves us.*

She sure does, I responded. *But why didn't Hanna?*

Perhaps she's otherwise occupied.

I didn't like the sound of that, especially since Carole was powerfully gifted and telepathically connected to so many others.

"Well, it seems we have a dilemma. We can only take two at a time, and we have to get ahead of the next storm. Who's in the worst shape?" asked another fireman — Bruce, according to his flaming-red name tag. He was short in stature and had a feisty temperament.

"Take Trixie and Carole first. I'll stay behind with Paige. Is that okay with you, Paige?" asked Allan. "We can stay together, and you can get some more rest before we make the trip out."

"Of course. Yes. Please take Carole and Trixie. They risked their lives coming here to rescue me. In fact, I insist." Relief set in as I did not want to be responsible for either one of my friends, in case anything troubling happened.

"But, Dad!" exclaimed Trixie. "I can stay with Paige. Remember, I helped save her from the grey wolf." She stood in defiance, trying to stare Allan down.

"Not a chance, Trixie. I'll look after her. You've done enough already. Help Carole back to her family. It's the way it should be. They'll be back to rescue us in no time, right guys?"

"As soon as we can, sport," Bruce replied. He saluted Allan and me.

Carole thought, *Paige, I should return to my dad and Uncle Kyle. They'll be worried, even though they should know I can take care of myself. Will you be okay, my friend?*

I answered, *Of course. But boy I've missed talking to you. We have so much to catch up on.* Carole nodded at me.

"So this is how we do it. We have snowshoes for you to put on." Bruce motioned to his colleague to retrieve them. "Step into them and we'll walk you to the ridge. Then I'm roping you two off, one of us ahead of you with our gear and one of us behind you. We'll scale the ridge in tandem. We have secured a rope ladder for us to climb. I have gloves you can use that have a non-skid surface so you won't lose your grip. Sound good so far?"

"Sure," replied Carole. "We've got this, right Trixie?"

I could sense Trixie was unsure as she looked at her dad, but she responded, "Yes, we do."

Allan hugged Trixie goodbye. "You can do this," he whispered.

I hugged Carole so tight; I hadn't realised how frightened I was. If anything ever happened to her ... She was my best friend, my irreplaceable BFF.

Then I heard, *No worries, Paige. We'll be fine. Don't forget Peggy's looking out for us too.*

She managed to calm me down a bit, but that was short-lived. I nodded as they left the cottage, but my heart jumped into my throat. I could barely swallow. Allan collapsed into the high-back wing chair and rubbed his head.

"Don't worry, Allan, they'll be fine," I said, not really knowing if it would hold true. It was the first time that I did not have a sense one way or the other as to the outcome of our rescue. It unnerved me.

"I'm going to go with that, Paige. I have to believe in the ability of the firefighters. I mean, they do this for a living, right? What are we so worried about?" he replied with a nervous laugh.

As soon as Allan finished speaking, I saw a flash of a moment when Trixie slips from the ladder. Bruce pushes her up and back on it. I thought it best not to share this vision with Allan. He was beginning to grow closer to his step-daughter, and I did not want to give him any cause to worry.

I left Allan and wandered to the kitchen to gaze out the back window, remembering the night that Dexter had tried to kill us. He had emerged from the forest looking like a zombie in search of flesh. Perhaps, in time, the memories would fade. Until then, I really needed to quit focusing on them. *Never give energy to past experiences,* floated into my mind. *Only the present moment matters.*

"Paige, help!" Allan cried, his voice cracking.

"What's the matter, Allan?" I pleaded as I rushed into the room.

I was terrified by what I saw. A horrid, translucent, dark energy bent over Allan, cackling and taunting him. It looked like a black figure with piercing, red eyes set into a wide face, with a crooked nose, and a forked tongue that flicked back and forth between shriveled lips. This was no spirit; I smelled sulphur and knew this was a demon.

"What is it, Paige?" Allan's eyes darted about in desperation.

It dawned on me that Allan couldn't see the demon. I stared into the dark being's red eyes and commanded as harshly as I could, "Leave him alone! Get out of here. Go now!"

The demon turned towards me and shrieked. When it spoke, its voice sent shivers down my spine. "How can you see me, mere mortal?"

"I banish you from this place!" I cried. "Go. Now!"

I had never seen a demon before, but I knew I wasn't alone in this encounter. I was being guided from Above. I could feel the loving embrace of my protectors as they helped me to expel the tainted spirit. The demon stopped laughing and, instead, stared in disbelief into my eyes.

"I said leave now, demon," I muttered in a low, guttural tone I barely recognized.

It disappeared before my eyes, leaving no trace of it ever having been in the room. Allan whipped his head to the side, hunched over, and vomited. He sat for a few minutes, got to his feet, and clutched me in a loving embrace.

"What was that? Was it really a demon?" he asked, hesitation resounding in his voice. "Could you really see it?"

I nodded. "I think I'm beginning to understand what Carole's so worried about."

My voice trailed off as I became lost in thought, trapped within my mind, analyzing the cause and effect of the evil zeroing in on us.

CHAPTER FOUR

Sometimes, it's unhealthy to remain lost in thought, isolated in your own little world. In fact, the last thing I heard Allan say was, "Paige, wake up!" And then I heard nothing at all, like a veil was thrown over my physical body, allowing my soul to elevate and become separated and then trapped within another dimension.

I wandered through a bleak, open field. Wind whipped across my face, turning strands of my hair into weapons — sharp blades that sliced at my face, causing tears to form in my eyes. I had no idea one could still feel their physical body while having an out-of-body experience. I was beginning to understand how the mind could play tricks, and I took it as a word of warning. *Careful, Paige, you may become what you think about most*, popped into my head.

Blackened, leafless trees stood tall, and looking closely, it was almost as if a face had been etched into each trunk. Two black holes for eyes, with their mouths painted in a grimace; it gave them an intimidating look. I was unsure whether or not they would become uprooted, spring to life, and attack me. As I steadied myself, readying for battle, I marched across the field and spied a dark figure approaching. As it drew near, I noticed wings — wide, black wings, the kind I assumed would be on a fallen angel. My worst fear popped into my mind.

No, it cannot be. God help me. Am I in hell? Fear overtook my mind until I heard a guiding voice.

Fight him, Paige! Fight him, the voice announced. *There is nothing to fear but fear itself. The demon feeds off lonely souls that give in to their fears. Think of your parents and how much you love them. In fact, think of the beautiful word 'love' and how many of your friends and family love you, as you love them. Feel it down to your soul. Say it, Paige. Say the word out loud: love! Now. It is your best defence against the power of the evil mind.*

A random song Mom sang when I was a young girl sprang to mind, and I began to sing the words, though I knew they weren't the correct ones.

"Love is in the air; I can feel it all around. Love is in the air. People love one another as one." The dark-winged creature stopped dead in its tracks, smirking at me. I continued. "Love is the Light. Love is the Truth. Love is the Answer to all that ails humanity."

The more I talked about love and revealed my connection to Above, the upperworld, the more the creature stepped back as if I'd punched him in the gut. I continued to speak— "The Light of God surrounds me. The Love of God enfolds me. The Power of God protects me. The Presence of God watches over me. Wherever I am, God is." He faded away. The prayer had been whispered into my right ear as I repeated it aloud, word for word. *Who is my helper?* It was mind-blowing. It was as if love and faith were the answer to fighting evil. *Could this be true? Could it be this simple?*

Yes, it is, said the voice. *Fear feeds demons and the fallen angels. That's how they prey upon people who are lost souls. They've become disconnected from their friends, their family, and their community. Demons wait in hiding until their chance appears. Then they enter the lost soul's body while they lie sleeping, or while they're in a fit of rage, and act out their hideous, hostile acts of betrayal. Once a body is commandeered, the demons can kill, steal, and become leaders who brainwash their followers, all the while camouflaged as human beings. Don't take this lightly, Paige. We are amidst a raging war between good and evil. The underworld is growing stronger, and they are bringing the battle to humans, on your plane of existence. If you are going to become strong enough to help Allan fight and annihilate the evil on the estate, you must overcome your innermost fears and never doubt your faith. Today was a test. You passed. But next time, will you be up for the challenge? This is a matter of life and death for your family and, eventually, for everyone in your world. I am the messenger sent from God.*

I slumped to the ground at the base of a tree. It astonished me to think that any of this could be true. I thought fairy tales were just that, not based in any truth. Dad used to read to me from The Brothers Grimms' fairy tales, and some of the stories were wretched. Even the original version of *Cinderella* was completely different from modern day versions. Cinderella's stepmom and stepsisters were pure evil. Could it be the Grimms wrote their personal experiences into their fictitious tales? Could Edgar Allan Poe have done the same thing? His poems had unravelled two mysteries upon the O'Brien estate. It made me ponder how very little I knew about the order of the universe.

Thinking back to my life in Scarborough, it seemed like a dream within a dream. Life had been so easy there, with no sightings of any spiritual activity except for my last day at my old high school, in the photo lab. It had all begun when Mackenzie walked down the corridor towards me. What did she have in her hands that day? It still haunted me. I often thought back to my first sighting of Mackenzie and wondered if knowing what she carried could've helped me now. Without thinking, I cried out, "Mackenzie, Conall, Archangel

Michael, anyone at all. Can you hear me?" I waited for an answer and eventually gave in to my exhaustion.

***

Sauntering through the woods, I sensed my friends' presence before hearing their laughter behind me. I felt like a young kid again. Tag was my favourite game, and I knew someone, perhaps my old friend Julie, chased me. I was a highly competitive person. I guess it came with the territory — an only child thing. So I broke into a run, and the safe, fun feeling transformed into a frantic game of cat-and-mouse as I tried to escape from my predator. My body dropped to the ground and out jumped my inner spirit wolf, Journey. I ran for miles with the sound of something running fast behind me, crashing through trees and bushes, crackling sounds with each footstep. And then I reached the edge of a cliff. Eager to blindly jump, I heard —

Stop! It's only me.

I turned around and came face-to-face with my friend, Blue-Eyes, the wolf with the grey fur and reddish highlights on his coat and behind his ears. My saviour on so many occasions. He was a beautiful sight to behold.

***

"Paige, I was so worried. You tossed and turned. And you're soaking wet from sweat. All I could think of to help was wiping your forehead with a cold cloth. I thought I'd lost you." Allan's eyes filled with tears.

"Wh-what happened? I think I'm losing my mind," I said. "You need to get me some help."

"'Scuse me, Paige. Don't you know where you are?" Allan asked, puzzled.

"We're in the old cottage … aren't we?" I asked. My left eye was glued shut, and a panicked reaction hit my gut.

"No, you're in the Camlachie Hospital, thanks to the firefighters who helped rescue us. When they returned a day and a half later, after the second storm front ended, you'd become unresponsive. Even the food and water Trixie left for us wasn't enough. I was going out of my mind trying to awaken you. Anyway, the firefighters had alerted the paramedics when the storm broke. They took you out through the cemetery path, on an ATV with a stretcher attached to a small trailer. It was the closest emergency route and a tricky rescue but you made it. We all did, together, Paige," Allan informed me. "Look around you. It's a hospital room. You have tubes coming out of you."

"Wait, what day is it?" I asked, pulling my fingers through my knotted hair.

"It's Sunday, April 3rd. It's a miracle, as Carole would say. On a Sunday, no less. And it's Easter! Easter Sunday." Allan smiled from ear to ear.

My brain caught up to my physical surroundings, and I realized Allan was right. I had no memory of the rescue or how I managed to end up in a hospital bed. *Ugh.* It was so narrow; I thought for sure I would fall out. It took my eyes a few minutes to adjust as I observed a doctor and a nurse rush in.

"Finally, you're awake! We've been so worried about you. It's been a week since you were admitted," said the nurse.

"Yes, we're all happy you're awake now, Miss Maddison," added the doctor as he grabbed my wrist and felt my pulse.

"And so am I," added a faint voice from somewhere nearby.

Slowly the curtain next to my bed was pulled back, and I saw a girl around my age. Her long, thick, black hair spilled down onto her hospital gown, and she was smiling at me, though her expression looked strained and unnatural.

"My name's Annie Ariana Booker, and I'm very pleased to meet you, Paige," she said in a husky voice. "Call me Ariana. I gotta say, you have some wicked dreams. I've been listening to you every night." She looked down at her arms and added, "I'm a cutter, myself."

I tensed at this admission and the nurse commanded, "You'll have plenty of time to talk to her later, Annie. Right now we have tests to run."

I heard the girl mutter, "For your information, Nurse Betty, it's Ariana, not Annie."

The nurse ignored her. She turned to me and said, "I'll let your grandparents know you're awake, and they can call your parents. Allan's been in touch with your friends Tracy and Carl ... or something like that. Now say your goodbyes, Allan. She's ours for now."

I smiled at the nurse, grateful for her concern, and thought Trixie and Carole would somehow find it funny about their new nicknames. I felt eyes upon me, and I returned Ariana's stare for a moment. As the attention turned away from her, I noticed a hateful expression on her face. She glared at the nurse, her eyes squinted and her lips twisted in a snarl. I made a mental note of it and turned over in my bed, struggling with the IV tube. Note to self: *Don't cross Ariana.*

CHAPTER FIVE

Later that afternoon, I asked my trusty nurse, Betty, to fetch Allan from the waiting room. She returned and shook her head; there was no sign of him yet. Bingo! I remembered I had finally managed to reassure Allan I was fine to be left alone for a couple hours while he picked up Trixie and Carole. My head was spinning as I tried to digest the recent events. Some alone time was probably well overdue. My physical body had been resting for days, but my mind hadn't been so lucky. I needed time to zone out and nap. Maybe I needed to sleep all day. I reclined my hospital bed and closed my eyes, ready for some z's. I had only a moment of rest before I was awakened.

"Paige, right?"

My eyes blinked open. The curtain was drawn between us. I rolled onto my side expecting the girl to draw the curtain, and whispered, "Yes, I'm Paige. Nice to meet you. Was it Annie or Ariana?"

"I go by Ariana, but the nurse insists on calling me Annie. I guess because it's my legal name. But call me Ariana." Her tone was firm.

A niggle in the back of my brain would not stop, and I tried hard to figure out what it meant. It was almost as if a soft voice was trying to grasp my attention, but it was being suppressed by something. I tried to ignore it.

"Ariana, mind if I ask you a question?"

"Ask away. Anything," she replied.

"What do you mean when you say you're a cutter?"

"Sometimes I cut myself ... on my upper thigh. You know ... with a razor blade. Long, shallow cuts. I started at the beginning of high school. I guess I was trying to make a point to my parents. The habit just sort of stuck."

I was a bit uncomfortable with the conversation, especially since we couldn't see each other. I felt bad for Ariana and wanted to help her, but I was over-the-top exhausted.

"I'm so sorry to hear that," I managed to say.

"Don't be sorry. Things happen. Bad things happen to good people; good things happen to bad people ... and the world just keeps on spinning."

I became wary of the conversation and was relieved when the nurse burst into the room.

"Annie, enough!" she said. "Let poor Paige sleep. She needs her rest!"

"My name is Ariana, Betty," came the cold reply.

Betty strode to my bedside and tucked the crisp hospital sheets under my sides, leaving me feeling like poor Mac McDonough, a caterpillar in a cocoon. She asked me if I needed anything, which I didn't, and then she strutted out of the room, leaving the door open behind her this time. I could feel thick tension between Ariana and Nurse Betty.

"Well, I guess I should let you sleep. I have my MP3 player to listen to anyway."

"Thanks. I am pretty tired," I replied.

Ariana's music drifted from her headphones — strange, haunted, instrumental music similar to that of a musician Mom had once discovered. I'd remembered his name — James Jandrisch — and searched the internet for him one day after mom had played his music on and off for weeks. He had created the music for a TV series named *Strange Empire*, a popular Western series. His music was not only haunting but intriguing as well.

No further words were uttered and I assumed Ariana had fallen asleep. It didn't take me long either, but it wasn't exactly a restful sleep. A deep sense of unease had settled into my bones, and I felt a chill despite the layers of blankets cocooning me. I thought I heard the suppressed voice again as I fell asleep, but I managed to shrug it off. Slipping in and out of consciousness, I heard footsteps echoing up and down the corridor, then whispers followed by animated conversations, and then nothing. Silence.

* * *

I felt giddy as I observed a heavyset nurse enter the room. She had wild, wiry, red hair. But when she flicked my wrist with her fingers and inserted a long needle into my arm, I cried out in pain. She chose to ignore me. Next, my forehead was poked and prodded with acupuncture needles, which seemed manageable enough until the doctor entered the room. He spoke sharply to the nurse and ordered more blood work. Great! She won't go easy on me ... again. As she tried to find a vein in my right arm, she swore under her breath about the lecherous doctor fooling around with an intern. And behind his wife's back, of course! I didn't want to listen to the gossip, but I was a captive audience. She finally switched to my left arm and squealed with delight when she found a vein. When she jammed the needle into my arm, the pain was excruciating, as if my nerve endings were exposed on the surface of my skin. I wanted to yell, I can feel this! *And though I tried, nothing came out of my mouth.*

How could this be? I can hear everything, see everything, feel everything, but I'm unresponsive? Just then, Allan burst into the room and had a heated discussion with the nurse. He exclaimed he had something important to tell me, and the nurse informed him that I was completely unconscious. But I could hear them talking about me. I'm here, I cried. There came no reply. Panic swelled within my body, and I struggled to get out of the narrow bed. As much as I tried to wriggle free of it, nothing happened. My body was unresponsive.

Allan seemed agitated, and I wondered what was happening. The curtain pulled back, and a girl stared at me. She had wild, green eyes, straight, long, black hair, and freckles, lots of freckles. She sat up in her bed and began to chant, moving rhythmically with her arms raised. She appeared to be giving me a blessing of sorts. As soon as the nurse turned around, the girl was lying flat-out in her bed. It was as if it had never happened. The nurse dismissed Allan with the promise to notify him first when I awakened. He ignored her, slipped over to the bed, put something into the palm of my hand, and curled my fingers around it.

***

I awoke to Ariana yelling at a new nurse. She was upset about the food; it wasn't vegan.

"Don't you know I only eat fruit and vegetables? No cheese, no meat. I may not have a family here supporting me, but I have my rights," she said.

My eyes slid shut once again, and I drifted in and out of sleep as Ariana continued to argue with the nurse. I noticed a young girl in a red smock slip into our room with a new plate of food a few moments later. She must have been the lunchtime volunteer. Ariana said something to me, but I didn't quite catch it as I succumbed to the land of dreams.

***

Suddenly, the hospital room turned pitch-black. As my eyes adjusted to the darkness, I noticed a thick mist pressed against the walls as if trying to escape. Then, an eerie red light appeared within the mist, illuminating my surroundings, and I heard chanting, faint at first, but growing louder. I could only make out one word malus *which was Latin for ... evil. I'd picked this up from mom when she studied for her final exam in an Introduction to Law course. Was someone chanting in Latin? Bizarre.*

I turned over onto my side to face the red light. A girl sat just beyond it, her face obscured by the darkness. I figured she was the one chanting, but her faintly visible mouth wasn't moving. The sounds seemed to be coming from all around the room, as if many people were chanting together. Soon, I noticed one pair of eyes and then a second, at least eight in all. A pair of dark figures swayed in every corner, and then they drifted towards the red light. I tried to scream, but I had no voice. Each figure was hooded, with only its eyes visible — deep, blood-red eyes that gave me the chills. I wanted to flee from the sterile room, but I was stuck in place like I'd been bound. The chanting intensified.

Allan burst onto the scene, causing the mist to disappear and the figures to shriek as they retreated into the shadows. A bright light filled the room, and, for a brief moment, I saw the face of the girl seated behind the red light. The girl's jet-black eyes reflected pent-up rage, and her lips were sewn shut. Her dark hair resembled straw, sticking up in every direction like she'd just been playing with a Van de Graaff generator in physics class. She seemed familiar.

***

Tossing and turning, I finally opened my eyes, and the first person I spied was the nurse who looked like a sentry standing guard over me. Allan stood next to her and held my hand as the doctor, opposite to them, prodded me with a thermometer. When the doctor noticed I'd awakened, he backed off and motioned to the nurse to join him by the door.

"Paige, how are you?" Allan asked, his voice quivering.

I frowned. The image of the girl's lips sewn shut was still burned into the recesses of my mind. *Why did she look so familiar?*

Allan seemed frantic. "Say something!"

"I'm fine," I mumbled. "What ... what happened?"

The doctor strode to my bedside and declared, "You had a seizure. Your vitals are normal. No spike in heart rate. Very strange, indeed." He tapped his fingers on my bedside railing. It irritated me.

"You screamed, too," added Allan. "I heard you as I sprinted down the hall."

Allan seemed really concerned. I reassured him I was okay and offered a strained smile. The doctor left without another word, but the nurse remained in place, staring at me with a puzzled look on her face. My smile faded. Her eyes reflected fear.

"Are you sure you're okay, Paige?" Allan whispered as he grasped my hand.

I nodded as if on autopilot, not knowing what to say. When I turned to ask the nurse a question, she bolted from the room, shaking her head and talking to herself as she left.

CHAPTER SIX

I had a troubled sleep that night, and it seemed to take forever for the wee morning hours to arrive. I awoke to see Allan reclined in the chair beside me, snoring. He must have spent the night diligently watching over me. I was grateful for him. My thoughts slipped to my other loving, faithful supporters—my grandparents, Carole, Trixie, Peggy, and Hanna. *Why haven't they stopped in?* I felt a slight tightness in my chest. Distracted by a tapping sound, I snapped my head towards Ariana and saw her banging her fingers on the bedside railing, listening to her MP3 player once again. She glanced in my direction, pulled off her headphones, and raised her right eyebrow at me.

"Hi there, sleepyhead. You've been out for a while," she said. "How are you feeling?"

"I still feel drained. I'd just like to go home and see my family and friends. I'm getting antsy staying here. These cold, sterile walls are not helping. And the smell. I can't stand the hospital smells—cleaning solutions most of all."

"I feel ya." Ariana's tone was kinder today. "It's really dull around here too. The nurse said I have to stay another night, and then I can leave. Oh, and I heard Allan talking to Carole on his cell. You'd better ask him about your fan club. When he wakes up, that is. He's a snorer."

"Okay, thanks," I said, sneaking a glance at Allan. "So what brought you in here, Ariana?" I felt more comfortable talking to her now, though I wasn't sure why.

"I overdosed on some pills last week. I wasn't trying to commit suicide like the doctors think; I just really can't sleep sometimes."

Ariana had a certain sadness to her that made me curious about her past. Clearly something bad had happened to her in her life.

"I have insomnia often," I said. "And I dream a lot. It gets exhausting. You know the dreams where you wake up with night sweats?" Allan stirred beside me but continued to snore. I giggled and turned back to Ariana. "Where's your family?"

Ariana hesitated. I was worried I'd been too blunt, but she finally replied.

"I was adopted."

"Oh, I feel like a fool. Sorry, Ariana, I didn't know."

"It's a long time ago, Paige. No worries. She was a single mom, a professor at the University of Toronto. I don't know much about her. I was given a box of photos from some of her archaeological digs. And there was no one else to take me. I ended up in and out of foster homes for several years until a young couple adopted me when I was seven. They were nice enough but rarely home. I was left with sitters most of the time. When I turned eighteen last month, I bounced here to Camlachie to get away from my adoptive parents."

"How come?" I asked, feeling shaky for being so nosy. I couldn't help prying, as though I was being nudged to continue asking questions. "I mean, why Camlachie?"

Ariana guffawed. "They were trying to use my inheritance money to pay off some of their debts. Like I said, they were nice enough. But they kept making bad business decisions and somehow justified it to themselves that by adopting me, and having control over my trust money ... well, let's just say they began to see it as their money too. I guess I was an easy source of capital."

"That's awful! How could they do that to their adopted daughter?" I looked away as tears formed in my eyes, and a sudden pang of remorse for Ariana hit me. My question about Camlachie remained unanswered, but I no longer wanted to pursue it.

"I don't really think they thought of me as their daughter. It was like adopting me was their charitable contribution to society. I stayed in their home. I ate their food. They bought me presents on holidays. But we almost never spent any downtime together, and they knew very little about my life. It's not like I had a troubled childhood or anything. I just really wanted to get away from them."

I was speechless, which was a first for me. I didn't know what to say to console Ariana. Hearing her talk about her life made me realize how thankful I was for my parents for all the loving, selfless support they had offered to me over the years. I missed them, and I wondered if my grandparents had called them in Italy to notify them of my misfortune. I didn't want them to worry about me but figured they should know.

Wait a minute! My grandparents ... where are they? I had a vague image of Grandpa visiting me in the hospital while I slept, but I wasn't sure if he'd actually been there or if it was just a dream.

"Paige?" Ariana's voice caught my attention. "Sorry. I know I tend to drone on sometimes." She lowered her head.

"No, I'm sorry Ariana," I answered, embarrassed that my thoughts had trailed off to my parents while she unravelled her heart-wrenching life story to me. "I was listening. My head's still a little bit foggy from all the sleeping."

Ariana laughed as she set her MP3 player on the table beside her. "So, what about you? I haven't seen your parents visiting. Only that handsome guy there beside you," she said with a nod in Allan's direction, "with his strapping body and piercing eyes."

I blushed. "Allan? Yeah, he's a ... a friend of mine. As for my parents, they're in Italy right now. I'm surprised my grandparents haven't been in to visit though."

"C'mon now, Paige. I think you and Allan have a thing." Ariana chuckled. "All right, I won't pry." She giggled and changed the subject. "Are you close with your family?"

"Yes, we're very close. I'm an only child, so I've spent a lot of time with my parents. Our family was estranged from my grandparents for almost seven years, but we recently moved in with them about a year ago." I stopped talking and wondered if I was being insensitive, considering Ariana's life story. Normally, I wasn't so open with strangers, but it was a relief to unload to a new friend. It felt strange that it was happening so soon, before we really knew each other. Yet, she was the only constant I had during my hospital impris-onment, and I felt I could lean on her.

"You sound like a loyal daughter and granddaughter. They're lucky to have you." Ariana gave me a rather odd smile and I noticed her sad eyes. "You know, I actually overheard the nurse mention something about your grandma. Maybe you should ask her about it."

Before I could reply, Allan sprang to life beside me. It was as if he had awakened from a nightmare. He grasped my hand. "I just had the weirdest dream," he confirmed.

"Paige Maddison?" an unfamiliar nurse said in a soft, warm voice as she entered the room and approached my bed. "I have some bad news, honey."

"Bad news?" I whispered, glancing at Allan.

"Your grandmother. She had a terrible fall. She's stabilized now and resting at your grandparents' estate, but I'm afraid she won't be leaving her bed for quite some time. It happened after you were brought in here. Your grandparents wanted to spare you the news until you felt better. They know you're on the mend, and your grandfather said he'll visit with you as soon as he can. He sends their love."

I felt a lump slowly forming in my throat. "Is she going to be okay?" I squeaked out.

"She's a tough lady," the nurse said with a smile. "I've known your grandparents over the years. I've been out to their big estate. She'll be fine."

"When can I go home? I'd like to help my grandparents."

"I'm sorry, honey, but you're not quite out of the woods yet," she said, her voice flat as she turned on her heels.

I was left feeling slapped. "Allan, will you please go and check on them for me? Please."

Allan looked around the room. The nurse was gone, and Ariana's headphones were securely in place, her eyes closed. "If you really want me to." He lowered his voice to a bare whisper and leaned in close to me. "But I think I should stay here with you, Paige. You never know what might happen to someone like you, or me, when we're most vulnerable. You know ... like you ... stuck here in the hospital. You're a sitting duck for ... you know. What's to stop them from attacking you here? Earthbounds ... er ... ghosts run rampant in places like this. They feed off the energies of those visiting in the hospital, the staff, and sometimes, the patients."

"Thanks, Allan!" I cried. "I really just need to feel safe right now."

Ariana ripped off her headphones and said, "No worries, Allan. I'll look out for Paige. Trust me." A Cheshire cat smile spread across her face and her eyes widened.

In my telepathic voice, I cried out to Allan, *How did she hear you?*

Allan seemed to ignore me and jumped up, nodded at Ariana, kissed me on the forehead, and announced he'd be back the next day with news.

I telepathically blurted, *No! Don't leave me here alone.* My heart pounded in my chest, and I broke out in a cold sweat, slamming my hands down beside me on my bed. "Wait, Allan! Where are Trixie and Carole, or Peggy and Hanna, for that matter?" My words fell on thin air. Allan had marched from the room, and his footsteps echoed eerily in the corridor as he retreated from the hospital.

After dinner, Ariana and I spoke a little more about her upbringing.

"My mom was an archaeologist and a mythologist who studied witchcraft in ancient cultures. She was especially intrigued by King Solomon. He lived in the 10th century, BC. You know, the son of King David. Do you know your Bible, Paige?"

Witchcraft had always given me the heebie-jeebies, and I guess it was because I knew little about it. I wasn't well-versed on the Bible, either. I shook my head and said, "Nope. That's not something that came up much in our family. The Bible I mean. It's only recently that a more spiritual connection has entered my life."

"Interesting. Since your move to O'Brien Manor?"

The conversation and Ariana's enthusiasm made me uncomfortable. "Yes, seems so," I said.

"Well, King David ruled the people of Israel, and he had a son, a prophet, named Solomon. David was pure of heart, so he was entrusted by God to govern the people, and He expected Solomon to do the same with a purity of heart. Solomon was the third king to rule Israel and the last before it split apart into smaller nations. According to rumour, Archangel Michael gave Solomon a ring called the Seal of Solomon. The ring was blessed by God and would help Solomon to enlist spirits to build the first temple and a wall surrounding the city of Jerusalem to protect them against evil. The Seal of Solomon was made of brass and iron, and the bevel was square with the Hebrew initials for God engraved upon it—one diamond and a hexagram representing the Star, or Shield, of David. It holds the key to all magic in the world, as it was empowered by Archangel Michael so Solomon could help protect his people from the actions of demons. And he could also control them." Ariana stopped to catch her breath, a devilish grin on her face. "Well that's enough about me. What about you? Do you know any secrets of the world?"

"Nope. That's an interesting story, Ariana, but I think I'm ready for sleep."

I rolled over and started to doze off as I heard the clunk of Ariana slamming her oversized headphones on. My mind raced with her story of King Solomon. His name played over and over in my mind. I tried to block it out by singing one of my favourite songs, one mom and I used to sing together, Michael Jackson's "Thriller." *Darkness falls across the land; The midnight hour is close at hand.* The words popped into my head, and I remembered it was actually the horror actor Vincent Price's verse in the song. A chill rushed through me as I nodded off.

When I awoke, I was relieved that no dreams had plagued me, but it was a brief, restless sleep nonetheless. Ariana was hunched over a peculiar-looking book that barely fit in her lap, illuminated by a clip-on book light. She was writing notes in the margins with an intense expression on her face. The book was leather-bound with what seemed to be bones lining the binding. Not wanting to alert Ariana, I gripped the bed railings and tried to pull myself upright without making a sound. As soon as I looked over, Ariana flinched and placed the book on the night table next to her bed. We made eye contact for a moment, and I caught a brief glimpse of anger. Her expression faded and she smiled.

"Sorry, Paige, you startled me," she said. When I didn't immediately reply, she added, "That's my diary. I'm a bit sensitive about other people seeing it."

"That's a ginormous diary."

"Yeah." Ariana chuckled. Maybe I had misread her expression; Ariana didn't seem angry at all. "It was my mother's. She found it in Jerusalem when she was travelling. Or at least that's what my adoptive parents told me."

"It's rather unique."

"Yeah, it's a bit creepy, isn't it?" Ariana laughed again, a joyful sound. "It reminds me of my mom, though, so I write in it every day. It's like there's a little part of her still with me, guiding me on my rightful path."

I smiled at the words she chose: rightful path. "It's not creepy. It's nice that you have a piece of your mom." I did not want to judge the one and only important legacy Ariana's mom had left behind for her.

We chatted well into the wee hours of the morning. Somewhere in the midst, I was comforted by a telepathic message from Allan, informing me he had been out to dinner with Carole and Trixie. They shared a laugh over their new nicknames, and they were happy to help out my grandparents while I rested up. I choked up for a moment at their thoughtfulness, realizing just how much I missed them.

Tiring, I bid Ariana a good night and yanked at the curtain to close it, only to notice my favourite multicoloured striped sweater tucked under her sheet. Ariana pulled up her covers and gave me a weak smile as she helped to close the curtain. It was an awkward exchange. Perhaps I had imagined it. I needed some z's before the sun rose. As I descended into slumber, I had the strangest waking dream. I had a vision of Ariana singing to me. It made me feel like all the worry in the world was melting away, until I heard voices shouting in the back of my mind. Too tired to care, I paid them no attention once again. I felt a strong bond with my new friend, and no one was going to come between us. I needed a friend.

CHAPTER SEVEN

Allan stormed into my hospital room as he announced, "Great, you're up. I've got good news! They're releasing you. I overheard the nurses talking, and they said you're okay now. Your grandparents send their love. I phoned them already and told them not to worry, because you'll be home later today." He paused to examine my expression and then added, "They're fine, Paige. Wipe that frown off your face."

I relaxed a little after hearing my grandparents were okay. As happy as I was to finally be going home, I noticed Ariana's bed was empty. *Did I miss her dismissal while I slept?*

Allan solved the mystery for me. "Ariana's downstairs getting an x-ray or something. You need to worry about yourself, Paige. Besides, this is the best day ever. Wait till Trixie and Carole see you! Not to mention Hanna, Peggy, and your grandparents. They can't wait to hug you. Would you be up to seeing our friends at O'Brien Manor? I know they're eager to welcome you home."

"Of course, Allan. I'm dying to see them."

Still, I couldn't stop thinking about Ariana. It was weird for me to focus so much on someone I'd just met, especially when my friends had probably been worried sick about me. I wanted to show them I was much better, though being the centre of attention was never my favourite thing. I was usually the one worrying about and taking care of others.

The tall, slim nurse who had informed me about Grandma's fall strutted into the room. A shiver ran up my spine. Did she have more bad news?

"Okay, honey. I guess the doctor says you're fit. You can go home as soon as the paperwork is done." She forced a smile.

"What time will that be?" Allan asked as he moved closer to my bedside and held my hand.

"Relax, Romeo. It'll be about an hour or so. I'll try to get the primary nurse on your case — you know, Betty — to speed up the process." Again, she turned on her heels and marched from the room.

"She's a strange one, Paige, but no matter. You're getting out of here today!"

"But where's Ariana? I want to say goodbye. Is she okay, Allan? There's something —"

"Hey! You missed all the fun today, Paige," Ariana said as a nurse wheeled her into the room. "I fainted a couple hours ago while you were sleeping. The doctor got all worried and sent me down for tests and an x-ray. It was a bit scary but I'm okay now. How about you?" She turned to the nurse and said in a flat tone, "You can go now. I'm fine. I can look after myself." The nurse huffed and strode off.

"I'm being released soon. I'm so glad I got to see you before I leave." I flashed a timid smile at Ariana. I don't know why I felt so shy around her, but I sensed she had more confidence than I did.

"Oh, I see."

A shadow crossed Ariana's face and her eyes seemed to darken as she stared at me. She looked disappointed. Her freckles seemed to join together as one big freckle on her cheeks. Now, she looked annoyed.

"Well, that's the end of our friendship," she noted.

"Wait, what? Oh no, I'm sure we'll see each other again, Ariana. Where did you say you're living? Maybe we can meet up—"

"Sure, but for now we have to get you home," Allan said. "I'm going to chase down that nurse." Allan shot Ariana a glare that surprised me.

"Remember, I told you ... or maybe I didn't. Funny story. I'm living with a single mom named Sarah. Her son moved out. He's at university now. Weird name she calls him— BAPS. I'm sure we'll see each other. When you're ready, Paige. Hey, pass me your cell phone."

A thud landed in my gut. I obliged Ariana and she added her cell number to my contacts list. Learning that she was now living at the home of my ex-boyfriend, Bradley Adam Parkman, disturbed me somehow.

"Don't forget, it's Ariana not Annie. That nurse Betty gets on my nerves."

Just as Ariana spoke, Betty entered the room. "What was that, Annie? I'm surprised Paige got any rest with you around. Up at night, reading from that book of yours. What are you doing with it, anyway?"

Ariana mumbled something and made an excuse that she had to use the restroom down the hall. The nurse and I exchanged a surprised look. *What's wrong with the bathroom in here?* I dismissed the thought and was elated to finally be going home.

***

"Surprise!"

As I crossed the threshold of O'Brien Manor, there stood my besties, Carole and Trixie, Grandpa, Hanna, and Peggy. I was thrilled to see all of them. It startled me to realize just how much I had missed them. Tears streamed down my face.

"I ... I don't know what to say, but I'm so relieved to be home again! Thank you, everyone, for being here. What would I do without you? I am blessed." *Blessed? Wait, when did I start using that word?* "It's wonderful to be home again. Can you please excuse me for a minute so I can see Grandma?" I asked, overwhelmed by all the attention. "I just need to see for myself that she's okay."

Grandpa marched over and held out his arm to me. "C'mon, Paige. She's been waiting for you. So impatient, she is. She's worse than your mother." Grandpa gave me a kind smile. His thick white hair, chestnut-brown eyes, and ruddy complexion gave away his Celtic roots. "And don't worry; I've let your parents know you're fine now."

I stumbled for a moment and was relieved Grandpa had a hold of me. "Must be all the resting in bed, Grandpa. Don't worry, it's nothing."

"Paige, you've been through a lot. Your grandmother and I have been praying for you to heal. It's always out of our hands until the Good Lord can help."

I gave his hand a gentle squeeze. How lucky was I that we moved to what I once called "Hicksville" but now was my cherished home in Camlachie? I regretted making fun of it and loved every bit of the small town feel and kindness shown, and I was even growing accustomed to the strange energy on the estate.

"Look who's here, Helen. Our dear Paige at last," Grandpa said, as we entered Grandma's bedroom.

She lay in bed facing the window and seemed to be asleep. I put my index finger to my lips and snuck around her Queen Anne bed. Her face looked peaceful, with her curly, fiery-red hair perfectly arranged like she had just been to a beauty salon. It comforted me to watch her breathe, her chest slowly rising up and down. It still took some getting used to—Grandma in her room and Grandpa in his own bedroom down the hall. But they were happy together after all these years. I motioned to Grandpa to leave me with her and plopped into her rocking chair, watching over her like the day she did the same for me after one of my spells. It happened on the first night I stayed in O'Brien Manor, and I had not forgotten it. The nightmare ... the one where I first laid eyes upon the hellhounds. Ten pairs of yellow eyes. Boy, how I wish that dream had never sprung to life!

I put my feet on the ottoman, closed my eyes, and rocked back and forth. It was wonderful to be home again.

"Paige, is that you?" Grandma whispered as she tried to sit up.

I snapped to attention. "No, Grandma, don't. It's not good for your hip. I'll go get Grandpa."

"Wait. Before you go, Paige, I want to say what a nightmare you've been through. We've been worried sick about you. How did you manage to survive at that broken-down old cottage? It's a miracle you're alive." Her voice trembled as she spoke.

"No worries, Grandma. Remember, I come from a strong gene pool. I'm a hardy O'Brien underneath it all."

Grandma laughed. "And don't forget my side of the family too, Paige."

"Actually, you've never told me your maiden name, Grandma. What is it?"

"MacIntyre. I thought you knew. Did you know in Scottish Gaelic it means the son of a carpenter or mason? Oh, no matter. What kind of grandmother am I? I've barely mentioned my family."

"Later, Grandma. We'll have lots of time as we recuperate together," I exclaimed as Hanna barged into the room.

"Let me fluff your pillows so you can sit up, Helen." She turned to me as she hoisted Grandma up onto the mountain of pillows and said in her high-pitched voice, "Paige we're so happy you're well and home for good. Don't ever do that again. I caught the dickens from your grandparents for letting you go in the first place. At least I packed you a first aid kit. Did it come in handy?"

"You betcha, Hanna. Boy, I've missed you guys." Hanna stormed over to me and hugged me so tight I lost my breath for a moment. "Okay, go easy on me now."

Hanna stepped back. Her hazel eyes glazed over. She had a plump, pale face, and high-top, grey-haired bun. "Sorry, Paige. I thought I'd never see you again. And when I did, I thought you'd never forgive me. I should've protected you, not let you set out by yourself at that time of year with the spring weather so unpredictable." Hanna looked away.

"Hanna, you couldn't have stopped me if you'd tried. You know I would've snuck out. I'm a bit strong-minded, but somehow I think it runs in the family," I laughed.

Grandma rolled her amber eyes at me. "You can say that again. You're just like your mother. Have you called her yet?"

"Should I? It's probably well after midnight in Monterosso al Mare, don't you think?"

"Your parents won't care, Paige," said Hanna. "They're anxious to hear from you. Call them. I'll sit with your grandmother."

I noticed the more respectful reference to Grandma. I wasn't used to Hanna and Grandma getting along. Perhaps they had put what I assumed to be their jealous rivalry aside during this stressful time. Normally, they competed with each other, especially for Grandpa's attention.

Exiting Grandma's room, I glanced across the hall into the bathroom where I had once found Grandpa collapsed on the floor. I forced myself to shake off the painful memory and hurried down the hall to the kitchen to use their landline.

"Paige, there you are. Come ... Peggy wants to talk to you and so do I," Carole said, as she sauntered into the kitchen, her soft-brown eyes reflecting the warmth of her soul. She placed her hand on my arm.

"I will, but I've been ordered to call my parents. Give me a minute, and I'll be right in," I said.

Carole turned on her heels, nodding as she left. I had really missed her and our last conversation flashed through my mind. She'd warned me that we were in grave danger again on the estate. I grabbed the portable phone and dialled the number taped to the side of the landline.

"Hello?" Mom mumbled, sounding sleepy. "Paige, is that you?"

"Mom, yes, it's me. I'm okay and I'm home now at the manor. Oh, I miss you and Dad so much." I began to cry.

Dad chimed in. "Paige, you're okay! We've been so worried. Thank goodness you called. We've been putting off sleep hoping the phone would ring. Haven't we, honey?"

It made me so happy to hear the love in my parents' voices. Whatever troubles they'd had on the estate had seemed to vanish. Finding out mom was a spirit wolf like me must have been shocking for dad and a deal breaker in most marriages. Our Celtic ancestry was a gift that kept on giving.

"I'm so glad you're together, Mom ... Dad," I said.

"Oh, dear. Your dad and I have been through lots of ups and downs in our lives, and we always stick together. Nothing will ever come between us."

"No, of course not. I love your mom now and forever, Paige. Never doubt it. We love you, and we're grateful for Allan. I hear he's watched over you since the cottage ordeal. What would we have done without him? And your grandma had her fall, but Grandpa's there to help— and Hanna too. Plus your friends, of course. And don't forget Peggy. I understand she's the one who wouldn't let the firefighters off the hook until they rescued you," Dad said.

"Oh my! I haven't even said hello to her yet." And as I spoke the heartfelt words, I felt eyes on the back of my head and turned to see Peggy standing in the kitchen doorway with an understanding smile on her tired face. She walked back into the living room.

"When are you coming home? Soon, I hope."

"Thankfully, your grandparents and Hanna can look after you until my responsibilities as the locum doctor are complete. Remember, Paige, I signed a contract, and I have to be here for the chiropractor until the end of June. His mother is still recuperating."

"We're really sorry, Paige. We wish your dad could get out of this, but we will see you as soon as we can," Mom said with a cheery tone. "It's only a few more months. I have a story I have to finish for the local newspaper."

I could not wait to see my parents. "Okay, then. Well, you two should be sleeping, and you probably have to work tomorrow, so I'll say good night for now. Thanks for picking up."

"No need to thank us, Paige. We're your parents! You can call us anytime. Good night, Paige," Dad said.

"We love you, Paige," cried mom.

Just as I was about to say goodbye, the phone went dead. I was upset that I couldn't add how much I loved them. I hesitated before joining everyone and glanced out the bay window overlooking the rose garden and the weathered fountain. The roses had begun to grow, and the forest was greener than before my trek to the cottage. Spring seemed to have sprung. On this thought, I heard, *Spring has sprung, the grass has ris', I wonder where the birdie is.* A shiver ran up my spine, and I darted for the living room.

As I approached, I spied Peggy waiting for me in the next room, the dining room. I darted towards her, and she took me by the hand.

"Paige, I've been so worried about you. I'm so thankful the firefighters took my worrying seriously and believed me that you were trapped at the cottage. I had a vision of you lying in a chair in the library. You looked unconscious to me. I kept sending you telepathic messages, but there was no response. Did you know I was sending you messages, dear?"

"No, I didn't receive them, Peggy. But oh, how I've missed you." I bent over and hugged her, reaching down to her frail, hunched-over body. Her voluminous, curly, white hair smelled of citrus.

"I've had visions of someone dark near you. Did you meet someone new, a new friend, perhaps?"

"Nope. I was trapped at the cottage. Carole, Allan, and Trixie came to rescue me until another storm hit us. They were snowed in with me. Then Allan sent them off with the firefighters. Could it be one of them?"

"No. But it does feel like a strong male energy. He, or she, is off a bit. You know, I cannot quite see if it's a male or female. There's a veil in front of the face."

"Well, I met a lot of people in the hospital, like nurses and doctors and such. And it wouldn't be any of my friends, like Allan, Carole, or Trixie." I searched her eyes for an answer. Then, it struck me. *Could it be Ariana?*

Just as I had that thought, Peggy sent me a tele-pathic *maybe.*

In my mind's eye, I had visions of Ariana helping me, looking out for me as I lay sleeping. Then I had a brief vision of her chanting and wondered if it was just a silly dream.

"It can't be Ariana, Peggy. I just met her, and she was so nice to me. She helped me in the hospital. If it wasn't for her friendship, I don't know what I would've done. My own friends weren't there for me."

It was out before I could take the words back. As I turned around, there stood Trixie and Carole. They just stared at me, mouths agape, and stormed out of the manor without saying a word. I felt terrible for defending someone I barely knew and compared her actions to my best friends, but somehow I felt connected to Ariana.

"Besides, Ariana is living with Sarah ... you know, Brad's mom. She's probably staying in his old room. Sarah wouldn't let just anyone live with her." I felt sickened as I spoke, but the harm was done.

"Paige, don't forget your true-blue friends. They're the ones who saved you and risked their own lives to find you." Peggy stopped and studied me. Her bright blue eyes penetrated my soul.

"I think I need to lie down now. This has been an overwhelming day. Can we speak again in a few days, Peggy? Please?"

Peggy lightened up and tapped my hand. "Of course, dear. You need your rest. I'll call you in a few days. I love you, Paige, like my own granddaughter. I ... well, we're all watching out for you. Don't you forget it."

I returned a weak smile and found my way to my bedroom, to my antique brass daybed. It looked inviting, but I felt riddled with guilt. *How could I have been so insensitive to say those things about my loyal friends? What came over me?* I rubbed my forehead as Hanna's footsteps echoed down the hallway towards me. I heard a slight pause in her movement and then it sounded like she turned back, perhaps to attend to grandma. I was left all alone with the moans and groans of a creaky old manor.

CHAPTER EIGHT

My heart ached that night as I thought about the way I had betrayed my two best friends. Though it was an exclamation shared with Peggy in the heat of the moment, the words were out there, my friends had heard them, and I couldn't take them back. I tried texting Carole and Trixie but there was no response. I understood they were hurt, and I understood the pain I had inflicted. They didn't deserve it, and a part of me wondered why I defended Ariana so adamantly.

With these thoughts swirling in my mind, I was hit with an acute case of insomnia. I gave up on sleep and surveyed my bedroom as shadows moved about, exposed by the light of the table lamp. It was my normal—watching shadows late at night. Nonetheless, I was grateful for the bedroom Dexter had fixed up for me, despite the cold hardwood floor. I had grown accustomed to the floral wallpaper, its bright red flowers and lime-green stems a perfect contrast to the curtains' loud green-and-red polka dots. It was over the top to have my own ensuite bathroom with its claw-foot tub and shower and gleaming white decor. I got out of bed and tiptoed over to the tiny bedroom window. The night was pitch-black, with no sign of the moon or stars. All was still; no wind whipped through the trees. I returned to bed and folded my hands upon my chest, remembering the first time I saw Conall in a dream, lying just as I was. So still. So ... And with that creepy thought, I slipped into slumberland.

***

A man with sun-kissed skin and expressive brown eyes spoke to me from beneath an ancient oak tree. His black hair was tied in two long, thick braids that spilled across the front of his tan, fringed clothing. I recognized him immediately as Grey Owl. He flashed a vision into my mind, reminding me of the conversation we'd once had after I was baptized in the babbling brook, when he'd informed me about my gift of second sight. It was given from our Creator, a gift to be honoured and heeded, not ignored. This time, his message was different. You are the watcher for your grandfather. Protect him and all living on the O'Brien estate. Families like yours carry secrets from past lives. *This is the message that haunted me the most.*

***

Upon awakening, I bolted upright, struggling to breathe; I felt like I was drowning. I grabbed my chest, trying to remember the breathing techniques I'd been taught back in Scarborough—the ones I knew would relieve my anxiety and help to center me. Breathe in through the nose and hold for a count of four; exhale through the mouth for a count of four. The vision of my baptism in the brook was so real; it felt like I had water on my lungs. One thing I knew for sure, when I dreamed like this, it was time for me to connect to the healing rock ... the grandfather rock by the brook. It was beautiful made of four colours: red, yellow, black, and white and it acted as a conduit between nature, our Creator, and our ancestors from the Light. Not only would I receive a healing but I'd also be provided with further information about messages that I'd received, or so I hoped. Note to self: *Ask Uncle Kyle for his interpretation of my dream.*

Lost in thought, I was jarred back to the present by the sound of something pecking at my window. I crept over to see what it was. A beautiful golden finch was perched on the edge of the framing and seemed to be looking at me as he cocked his head from side to side. I glanced at the digital alarm clock: 5:04. *Too early for me to rise*, I thought, until I received a message from Peggy.

Wake up. It's time to learn from Grey Owl.

It never ceased to amaze me how Peggy—or Carole, for that matter—seemed tuned into my thoughts. I knew I had to visit the babbling brook before anyone noticed my absence, so I scrambled to my closet to get dressed.

I headed for the manor's east entrance and slammed into Allan as I flung open the solid wooden door.

"What are you doing up so early?" I asked.

"Hey. Just checking on you. I never know if you're okay or not," he said, a look of loving concern on his face.

"I'm fine, Allan," I assured him.

"When you went missing, I promised myself I would be a better protector. Somehow, I was caught up in helping Trixie heal and forgot about you. If I had just been here that day ... the day you set out—"

"Stop it, Allan. It's not your fault. First of all, you're supposed to look after your stepdaughter. And second, I snuck by the guesthouse while the two of you slept. I purposely did not want you to know where I was going, and I didn't want you to follow me. I had a mission, and you know what I'm like. Kind of stubborn, I guess. Next time, I won't be so foolish, I promise."

Allan put his arm around my waist and drew me closer. "Paige, I'm not sure how much longer I can stop myself ..."

"Oh, you can. We promised not to be involved with each other until this war on the estate is over. It would cloud our judgement. Remember?"

As I tried to ignore the passion sparked by Allan's body next to mine, my thoughts raced to my poor grandma recovering in her bed. *Had the evil energy on the estate somehow caused her fall?* I wondered.

"You're right. So, where are you going now? May I ask?"

"I have a meeting with Grey Owl down by the babbling brook. But you can't come, Allan. I'm sorry. This is something I have to do alone." I broke away from him and smiled. "I'll text you later to let you know I'm fine."

"Okay. When will you be back?"

"I'm not sure, but you'll be the first to know."

I sauntered towards the path to the guesthouse and crossed the stone bridge. It was breathtaking to watch the brook wind beneath it, pooling here and there. I heard a splash and saw a Canada goose touchdown, and then I veered off the path. I walked alongside the guesthouse until I reached the portal to the forest — the portal that led to all things beautiful on the O'Brien estate. The ivy was beginning to wrap itself around the broken-down wooden archway. *I need to get Allan to fix this someday*, I thought. I rolled my eyes, wondering when I'd become such a homebody. I strode through the portal and screamed as a perfectly shaped spider's web covered every inch of my face. It had little bugs trapped inside its webbing. I danced around, screaming as I peeled it off. It was so gross. The encounter not only fully awakened me, but the creatures of the forest stirred too.

The sight of the chickadees flitting about calmed my nerves. I found their familiar call, *chickadeedeedeee,* to be endearing. Robins sang sweetly, and crows cawed overhead. They seemed to relax me, reminding me I was not alone. I jogged along the path that veered to my left, admiring the ancient, towering trees as they swayed around me. Being in the forest centered me. Just when I thought my morning couldn't get any better, I heard it: the sweet sound of the babbling brook. Oh, how I'd missed the gurgle of gently flowing water as it tumbled its way over the rocks below. And soon enough, I saw the clearing and the healing rock, but not before I spied Grey Owl. A surge of peacefulness enveloped me as Grey Owl waved and gave me his endearing smile. Finally, I was safe.

"Welcome, Paige. Happy you could come here as the birds awaken."

"Funny you should say that, Grey Owl. I was awakened this morning by a golden finch pecking at my window."

"Ahh. Perhaps the finch was sent from our Creator as your personal wake-up call," Grey Owl said as he chuckled. "It is necessary that we talk. I understand you've had some trouble. Carole's Uncle Kyle informed me, and he insisted that we discuss what's disturbing you. Please sit." He motioned to me to join him on a nearby log. "It seems you have a responsibility to carry out, Paige. Sometimes, we come into this lifetime knowing in our souls what we must do. You were born into this time with your parents, but no one could've prepared you for what is to come. You must remember to heal yourself with the healing rock. Remember to kneel and touch the rock. Take a few deep breaths, exhale each time, and then try to clear your mind and let the healing begin. Go ahead. I'll go for a walk while you do this. Whistle when you're done." And with that, Grey Owl strolled away.

I drew in a deep breath, counted to ten, and then slowly exhaled. I repeated this several times before dropping to one knee and resting my left hand gently on the rock. Nothing happened at first, so I tried to clear all worries—about my family, my friends, and Ariana—from my mind. But the thought of Ariana distracted me. I had a vision of her standing in the forest, observing me. I was startled at first, but then I saw Grey Owl walking towards where she stood. Ariana vanished. I went back to my breathing technique, and soon I saw the familiar face of the wise old man with the long, braided, white hair draped over each shoulder, and a white feather tucked behind his left ear. It was comforting to see him again, as he was one of my first spirit guides I'd received messages from. While I concentrated on his energy, he spoke.

Grey Owl will teach you many things about the spiritual world. Ask him about the story of the grandfather rocks. You need to understand the power at your fingertips. One day, you will use this power to battle evil. There is more to this world than meets the eye. Many unseen forces are at work—some on your behalf; some working against you. The answer lies within your soul, child. Remember to keep your thoughts positive, your heart full of love, and to trust your friends and family, the ones who've been with you since the beginning of this journey.

The vision ended when I heard a twig snap amongst the bushes. A cold sweat raged across my brow, and I fell away from the rock. I began to laugh when I saw a chipmunk run towards me. Grey Owl was back in a flash.

"Did you receive your healing, Paige?" he asked.

Grey Owl had a warm smile, and sometimes I did not want to break the silence while I studied his weathered face and sensed his trusting soul.

"Well, the wise old man with white hair and braids spoke to me. He called me child. And he gave me a warning and some words of advice. I guess ... I had my healing?" I still struggled to understand my experience.

"The warning was important, and you had some healing. Return again, Paige, when the forest is quiet. And keep returning until you feel in your soul you are healed. You'll know when that time comes."

"Thank you, Grey Owl. I'm grateful for your help," I said, humbled.

"Oh, I am the one who is grateful. Helping you along your path is my destiny. Human will dictates how each of us behaves. You don't have to allow me to help, but here you are. Thank you, Paige. You are listening to your spirit guide. Don't stray away from the messages you receive. I fear someone is trying to steer you from your destiny."

The last remark weighed heavily on my mind. Another warning about someone trying to hurt me. An image of Ariana flashed before my eyes, and I was just about to mention her when Grey Owl waved and turned to leave.

"I'll be here for you when you need me most. Just think of me. Goodbye, Paige, for now."

I bit my tongue and didn't say another word. I certainly didn't want to take advantage of Grey Owl. He was a busy elder, and I assumed he helped many. Still, the thought of Ariana in the forest disturbed me somehow. I tried to recall where Bradley Adam Parkman's house was located. It was to the east of the manor, about one and a quarter miles, if I remembered correctly. I never did visit his house, as he worked for my grandparents on the estate.

Approaching the manor, an unsettled feeling landed in my consciousness. Then it came to me. I forgot to ask Grey Owl about the grandfather rocks. Note to self: *Next time, have it at the top of my list of questions. What knowledge will I learn from them?*

***

What began as a warm, sunny day soon turned to clouds rolling in with a crispness in the air. The birds grew silent. The kitchen screen door creaked as I opened it, and there was

Hanna, busy baking in the kitchen. The pungent fragrance of blueberries wafted over to me.

"There you are, Paige. I was waiting for you to get up. Look! I've made your faves." Hanna waved the fragrance from the muffins under my nose. "I wanted to make you my scrumptious blueberry muffins! I'm assuming they didn't bake these for you in the hospital," she said in her high-pitch voice that cracked on the last word.

"They smell delicious," I said and slumped onto the kitchen nook bench. "You know, Hanna, you've been a gift to me. Sure, we've had our moments. Remember that day in the kitchen when I smashed the candy dish and you channeled the dark soul who had been haunting me? I know now from Grandpa that was out of your control. You've been here for me every step of the way on this journey of mine. And I never once thought you were at fault for letting me set out that day. You respected my wishes, and that made me feel loved. No one can predict the weather one hundred percent. Who knew it would turn from a sunny spring-like day to a full-blown winter storm?"

Hanna dropped the pan of muffins onto the speckled navy-and-white countertop, hurried over to me, and hugged me for dear life. "Paige, you've become a part of my family. Do you know that? I don't know what I'd do without you or your grandparents. Your grandmother and I finally understand one another, and I feel at home here. I've got no one else. Please don't ever do anything like that again. It's one thing to want to help, but to put yourself in danger is ... well ... irresponsible. And I enabled you. I'm a terrible mother figure. Good thing I have no children..."

I broke from her grip and looked Hanna in the eyes. "Don't say that, Hanna. You've been my rock since our move here. I won't do that again, I promise. And you're not a terrible person. There is something terribly wrong on this estate, and I am going to get to the bottom of it. You were used as a pawn in the ongoing battle." I feigned a smile, hoping I would be able to uphold my promise.

Grandpa walked into the kitchen, and I greeted him with a warm hug. "This is just the perfect day. I'm home and happy." Grandpa held me for a few more seconds.

"Well, there's someone waiting to see you. She's up and moving around her bedroom with her walker. Go to her, Paige," Grandpa said softly. His ruddy complexion seemed quite flushed, and I worried his health wasn't in the best state either.

I ran to Grandma's room and stopped before she saw me. I watched as she moved her walker with each hesitant step. She had a ways to go, but at least she was out of bed.

I barged into the room. "Grandma, it's wonderful to see you up and about!"

"Thank you, Paige. I feel the same way. It's because of you, dear. Now that I know you're safe, I can begin to heal. I was frightened that you were lost and worried we'd never find you. I didn't have the strength or will to even get out of bed."

I approached Grandma and laid my hand upon hers. "No worries, Grandma. I can take care of myself. Trust me."

She nodded. "And *that* I am beginning to believe. There's more to you than meets the eye, Paige Alexandra Maddison—in a good way."

I threw myself onto her unmade bed, the O'Brien quilt laying half on the floor. Then I thought better of it, got up, and neatly folded the cherished family quilt over her gold wrinkle-free sheets. I knew how much the family heirloom meant to my grandparents.

As I studied the quilt's embroidered coat of arms, I had a memory of the first day I saw it and Grandpa's explanation of what it meant. I traced the red shield with my finger, admiring its details: three lions, a sword-wielding arm coming down from the heavens, and the words *Lamh Laidir an Uachdar*—"strong hand from above" or "strong hand uppermost." I believed our family was meant to be that strong hand and defeat the earthbounds—those spirits of the dark whose anguished souls seek revenge and retribution—and to fight against demons, once and for all!

CHAPTER NINE

Each day, Grandma continued to improve. In fact, she was soon helping Hanna prepare some of our meals. I had never witnessed Grandma doing that before, but they often laughed together, revealing their newfound friendship. Grandpa seemed spry as he helped around the house, doing the dishes and even some vacuuming to relieve Hanna's workload so she could spend more time with Grandma. I rejoiced in knowing some good had come out of Grandma's fall and my error in judgement visiting the cottage at a volatile time of year with the weather. We all felt happier, lighter, and more peaceful living in O'Brien Manor.

***

Early one Saturday morning, I heard the clanging of the door knocker and wondered who would drop by before breakfast. Whispered greetings soon carried down the hallway to my bedroom. I had a flashback to the day Delia had arrived and informed my grandparents of Dexter's death. I shook it off, jumped into my fluffy pink robe and matching slippers, and peeked around the corner into the foyer. There stood Carole, arm in arm with her Uncle Kyle. The rainbow-coloured yoga suit she wore brought a smile to my face. As Uncle Kyle closed the oversized doors, I admired his leather vest, especially the wolf embossed upon it. I noticed he was—as always—well groomed, his tightly braided dark-brown hair reaching halfway down his back. But the look of concern on his weathered face told me this was a a serious visit.

"Paige!" Hanna yelled before she spotted me standing in the shadows. "Oh, there you are. You have visitors. Nice to see you both again." She wiped her hands on her floral apron then shook Uncle Kyle's hand and returned to the kitchen.

"I'm so happy you're here," I said as I peeked around the corner. "Hello, Uncle Kyle. Can you give us a few seconds, please?"

"Of course. I'll wait outside. Take your time." This time, I noticed a colourful feather tucked into the brown leather tieback for his braid.

"Paige, knowing you for as long as I have, coming up on a year, I know you didn't mean what you said to Peggy." Carole took my hands, and I noticed her usually tanned skin had paled, and her brown eyes were wide as saucers. "You probably aren't aware of this, but you were only allowed one visitor in the hospital, and Trixie and I felt it was best that it was Allan. For your sake. We thought you might be under attack again. Is it the earthbounds causing you trouble? Do you know?"

Then it hit me: Carole and I had never talked about what took place at the cottage or my stay at the hospital. "I haven't given it much thought. In fact, it's hard for me to remember what happened. I know I had visions of speaking to God—at least I think it was God—but I can't remember much about it. I woke up in the hospital, and they had me on an IV drip. I drifted in and out of sleep, but Ariana was always there, watching over me."

"Wait, the girl you mentioned to Peggy? Who is she?" Carole's brown eyes darkened and narrowed.

"Ariana? She was in the hospital bed beside mine. I don't know much about her, but she's living with Sarah, Brad's mom, at their house."

"You're kidding? Is his mom not expecting Brad to come home again? Don't you think that's strange?" Carole asked. "Maybe he really is afraid of what's happening on the O'Brien estate. I thought for sure he'd eventually return to help you ... us."

"Me too, Carole. Anyways, I'm sorry for what I said about you and Trixie. I didn't mean it. I was wondering why you never came by, but that was stupid of me. I should've realized ... Well, here we are together again." I smiled at Carole, and I could tell by the light in her eyes that all had been forgiven. Looking away, I said, "Ariana moved here to get away from her adoptive parents. She said they took her inheritance to finance their debts. Or something like that."

"Wow, that's terrible. No wonder you feel a bond with her. Staying at Brad's, and her estrangement from her adoptive parents, like your family was estranged from your grandparents. You have a lot in common."

"More than I realized. She's an only child too. Anyways, she watched over me at night, so I felt safe and could sleep. Although ..."

"What? What is it, Paige?" Carole asked with an urgency in her voice. "Spill it."

"One night, I woke up with a start, and she had a strange, oversized book in her lap, her 'journal' she called it, and she was writing in it. It had bones as the spine, holding it together." I scrunched up my face as I recalled it. "I'm not sure now if I really saw it or not. Maybe it was the meds."

"What else do you remember?"

"Oh, yeah!" I shouted, swatting her shoulder for emphasis. "I remember now. I heard chanting one night, and I saw a girl with dark hair and … and her lips were sewn shut."

"Gross. Maybe that was just a bad dream. Chanting? Maybe she was praying for you?"

"No, there was a red light, and, whatever was happening, the nurse walked in and broke it up."

"You'd better go slow with this new friend. You don't need any more trouble." Carole smiled and grabbed my arm. "Let's go. Uncle Kyle has lots to tell you."

"Wait, I'll get dressed and meet you outside," I yelled as I ran to my bedroom.

Uncle Kyle had moved to the flower gardens and was pulling some weeds. "You have to nurture your gardens, Paige. Don't forget to do this," he said, as I emerged from the manor.

"It's not really my thing," I said. "Besides, Allan is supposed to be looking after the grounds."

"Now, now, Paige. Careful. We are all responsible for nature and what's around us. It would be healing for you to help out—for your grandparents' sake. Come here and I'll show you how."

I trudged over and knelt beside him, and he showed me which weeds to pull out and which ones were helpful.

"See this two-foot weed? It's called butterfly milkweed. Remember it by its bright orange flowers. You can chew the fresh root for bronchitis. And these sunflowers are all over the estate. If you crush them up and make a paste, you can use them to draw out blisters. That'll help you the next time you go exploring on your own," Uncle Kyle chided. "Now, do you have your medicine bundle? It's time you learned of its power. I have lots to share with you."

"I'll be right back," I said as I scrambled into the manor without shutting the oversized double doors and raced into my room. For a moment, I could not think of where the bundle was until I calmed down and cleared my thoughts. In my mind's eye, I saw the bundle in a cherrywood box with a picture of mom and me wedged into the lid. I grabbed it from the back of my closet and met up with Uncle Kyle and Carole. I found them sitting cross-legged next to each other beneath a red maple tree to the east of the manor. They were laughing, and I hesitated to interrupt their intimate moment.

Uncle Kyle motioned for me to join them, and I plopped down next to Carole.

"Great, Paige. Now, say your prayers—the ones that mean the most to you. Carole, we'll bow our heads in silence. Once you're done, you can take the medicine bundle out of the box."

I began to recite Psalm 23:

> *The Lord is my shepherd, I shall not want.*
> *He maketh me to lie down in green pastures:*
> *He leadeth me beside the still waters;*
> *He restoreth my soul:*
> *He leadeth me in the paths of righteousness*
> *for his name's sake.*
> *Yea, though I walk through the valley*
> *of the shadow of death,*
> *I shall fear no evil: for thou art with me;*
> *thy rod and thy staff they comfort me.*
> *He preparest a table before me in the*
> *presence of mine enemies:*
> *He anointeth my head with oil;*
> *My cup runneth over.*
> *Surely goodness and mercy shall follow me*
> *all the days of my life:*
> *And I shall dwell in the house of the Lord,*
> *for ever and ever. Amen.*

When I finished, I opened my eyes and was surprised to find us seated together in a triangle, legs crossed.

"Would you mind if I said The Lord's Prayer also?" Uncle Kyle and Carole nodded, bowing their heads in silence again. I began:

Our Father, who art in Heaven,
Hallowed be thy Name.
Thy kingdom come.
Thy will be done,
On earth as it is in heaven.
Give us this day our daily bread.
And forgive us our trespasses,
As we forgive those
Who trespass against us.
And lead us not into temptation,
But deliver us from evil.
For thine is the kingdom,
And the power, and the glory,
For ever and ever, Amen.

I reached into the box and gently retrieved the colourful medicine bag with its green crosses and geometrical pattern of beige, brown, turquoise, yellow, and black weave. Holding it made me feel warm in my heart. I awaited Uncle Kyle's instructions.

"Now open the bag and put it to your nose. Inhale the contents. Remember, it contains sage, tobacco, cedar, and sweetgrass from Mother Earth, so it should help you breathe easier. I know you've been having some troubles, Paige. Anytime your breath runs short, open the bag and slowly breathe in the contents. It will help to heal your whole body. Don't let anyone else see or touch this bag, other than the three of us, okay?" Uncle Kyle said, his tone firm, but gentle.

"I promise, I won't," I replied, tucking my curly locks behind my ears.

"Once we created and had the medicine bundle blessed ... well, let me explain. We asked many elders to help with this spiritual request. Some came from far away. We're all Ojibwe but we live on different reserves. Some elders came from the east of Orillia, some from Christian Island, and most elders were from our band. Once I blessed you and gave you the bundle, you became a spiritual member of ours. We are tied to you now, and you are tied to us. Many of your visions have been aided by our ancestors. After all, you and Carole are sisters now." He smiled at Carole. "You two must look after each other. Your bond is stronger, like none other. And I'm happy to hear you call me Uncle." He winked at me.

I beamed as he declared I was family. As a child might do, I reached out my pinky finger and said to Carole, "Pinky swear. Now we're bonded for life." We locked fingers for a moment before breaking our hold with lighthearted laughter.

I had to admit, after inhaling the contents of the bundle, I felt empowered, physically strong, and ready to take on whatever dark elements crossed my path. I remembered the first time Uncle Kyle explained it to me, after Hanna's possession. Her black eyes haunted me for a moment, but the memory faded as I focused on the medicine bundle. I was honored that a group of elders I didn't know had gone to such great lengths for my health and for my family's welfare. As significant as it was that I had so many supporters, I couldn't help but feel a twinge of paranoia. *Why do I need so many supporters and so much healing? What is coming?*

I snapped back to the present moment. "Indeed, I will look out for Carole. She sure does so for me. More than I probably realize."

As soon as that was said, I had another vision of Ariana. She looked angry. I saw her in Brad's old bedroom tossing a pile of books off the bookshelf and swearing aloud. I couldn't figure out why I was getting these visions of Ariana. *Was she sharing her emotions with me? Or was someone else sending me visions of her as a warning?*

Uncle Kyle interrupted. "I know you're beginning to understand that your new friend … well, she's not to be trusted."

The comment put me on edge. I knew Uncle Kyle would not make such a statement lightly, but something about Ariana struck a nerve in me and made me defensive about her.

"I promised Carole I would take the friendship slowly. I promise both of you."

Uncle Kyle didn't say another word. His eyes dilated and he grabbed his chest. "I have to go now. Be careful, Paige." He arose and stormed away.

"What was that all about, Carole?"

"I dunno. I better go after him. Remember what he said. I love you, Paige, like a sister. Don't you forget it. I'd do anything for you." She scrambled to her feet, dusted herself off, and darted after her uncle.

CHAPTER TEN

It was time to face the music. I dragged myself into Camlachie High and knew my past was about to catch up with me. Standing next to my locker was Carole, and next to her was our principal, Ms. Halfourd, dressed in her navy blue banker's suit. She was average height, with a blonde bob haircut. Her square, thick-lensed, black-framed glasses perched on a tiny nose above pencil-thin lips. If we were playing poker, her stoic look would do nothing to give away the four aces in her hand. I felt like I had to visit the bathroom, but it passed. It was time to answer for the classes I had skipped, on and off, throughout the school year.

"Paige, we're happy to see you, and you look well, too. We're all so sorry that you were trapped at your grandparents' old cottage. How did you survive the ordeal?" she asked.

It was not what I expected to hear. Taken aback, I studied her face for a clue that this was a ruse, and she was truthfully quite unhappy with my attendance at school and was ready to bust me for it. *Could I be wrong?* I went with it.

"Thank you for your concern, Ms. Halfourd. I was lucky that our neighbour, Peggy, called the police and alerted the fire department. But my friends arrived first to rescue me, and then another nasty winter storm blew in, unfortunately.

In spring, no less. Then firefighters and paramedics rescued us, and I ended up in the hospital to recover. I'm rested and ready to come back to school." I forced a smile but wondered where the conversation was headed. "That is, if you'll allow me to." I flinched, not really wanting to know her answer to my request.

"Carole tells me you've also been looking after your ailing grandfather, and your grandmother recently had a fall. That's a lot for a young girl to handle. I understand your parents are away in Italy? Anyhow, her Uncle Kyle vouched for you too." She paused and studied me for a moment. I tensed up a bit. "I guess we all misjudged you, Paige. Your teachers and I thought you were skipping school — yet another rebellious teen. Despite your absences over the past year, somehow your grades have been consistent ... except for your calculus and chemistry grades. I've reassessed my original recommendation to the school board. If you repeat those two classes in summer school, you'll satisfy me and the board and pass your final year. You've only missed one assignment in each of your classes this term. Lucky for you, your friend Carole encouraged you to complete your assignments early. You'll be good to go to university next year, if you wish. You've been a brave soul, Paige. We feel you've experienced enough trauma for one year. Well, I best get back to work now. My, my. You just never know about people, do you? Enjoy your day, Paige. Carole." She tucked a file underneath her arm and marched off like she'd won an award or something.

I fell against my locker. My eyes widened as I exclaimed, "Carole, I'm shocked. What did you and Uncle Kyle say to her? I thought I'd be expelled and have to redo the whole term. Not that I'm thrilled with repeating chemistry ... ugh. Or calculus. But I'm pretty lucky."

"Let's just say Uncle Kyle has a way with words. He argued with Principal Halfourd for over an hour. He didn't back down, not once. And neither did I. You're a hero, Paige. Look at what you've done for your grandparents. They're healthy and happy. There is no sign of any earthbound, hellhound, or anything else on the estate. Grey Owl feels you are healing yourself. And you overcame your experience at the cottage. Those are lessons that cannot be taught in school. I look up to you; I really do." Carole said, beaming. "Well, we'd better get to class before Ms. Halfourd changes her mind."

"Not before we have a hug," I said. Carole wrapped her arms around me and squeezed hard. For a moment, I was unable to breathe. "Okay, Carole, I know. We all dodged a bullet this time around. But we had better get to class or my next teacher may not let me in."

We sauntered down the hallway to Mr. Higgins' music class. He didn't like me much, and I really felt like running away. Carole nudged me into the room and then moved on to her physics class.

Glad that one's behind me, I messaged to Carole. She turned around and messaged me, *Thanks a lot.* Then she giggled.

Mr. Higgins didn't waste a minute. "Well, well, here she is. We've been waiting to welcome you back, Paige. Haven't we, class? Say hello, everyone."

My fellow students gave me a resounding "welcome back" in unison. I felt like I was in elementary school again. I nodded and flopped at my desk near the back of the room.

"Oh, no, Paige. We have a special desk for you up here, at the front of the class. Come now." He clapped his hands. "Ginger has offered to give up her desk and to help you catch up on your studies, haven't you Ginger?"

She nodded slowly, and strode to the back, her blue eyes blazing. Ginger broke into a smile and whispered, "Gladly. I hated being at the front of the class. Thank you."

"Thank you, I think," I whispered in reply. She flashed me a smile.

For the remainder of the class, it felt like Mr. Higgins was speaking Latin. We were reviewing elements of music theory that had been taught over the course of the semester. Having missed almost six weeks' worth of classes, I could barely follow the lesson. I found the red elastic band I'd tucked into my backpack earlier and placed it on my wrist. I knew I'd feel panicky today, and snapping it on my wrist made me feel less anxious.

The bell rang and Mr. Higgins asked me to stay behind. "I don't know what happened to you, but I did get my orders to assign you one last project so you can complete this class. I'm not sure how you manipulated Principal Halfourd, but I have to do as she suggests. Here it is. You can take the file home and look it over." He sat at his desk and refused to look up at me or answer any questions I might have.

My next two classes were French and social science. They went better than with Mr. Higgins. Both teachers empathized with my disappearance and my recovery. I guess it helped that they knew my family. My social science teacher, Mrs. Defray, had gone to school with my mom. Her assignment for me was to write a paper describing the changing views of psychodynamic theory in modern psychology. My French teacher, Madame Clouthier, assigned a paper analyzing the use of metaphor in Edmond Rostand's *Cyrano de Bergerac*. Mom had read it once and loved the sincerity of Cyrano's poetry, written from his heart for the love of a woman he felt he could never have due to his awkward appearance. In the end, the inherent message rang true to Mom: true beauty comes from deep within, from the soul.

Seated alone on the elongated couch in the living room after supper that night, I opened the file from Mr. Higgins. *Such a peculiar man.* I found a sealed envelope with my name and the word *Confidential* scrawled across the front. A handwritten note was folded inside.

Dear Paige, Your friend Ginger informed me that you've been helping to look after your ailing grandparents. She said that's the reason you've missed so much school. If this is true, then I feel you've completed my class. I know some of your family history. I had your mother in my class many years ago. Lori, isn't it? I have to agree with Principal Halfourd, and I feel you've been through enough. I heard about the cottage and your stay in the hospital. Good thing Ginger is also looking out for you. She's my top student. It was most unexpected from her... to come to your aid. I didn't even know you were friends. Cheers, Mr. Higgins.

Once again, another person ran to my defence. But Ginger? I never took the time to get to know her. And it made me wonder what she knew about my family. I was overwhelmed for a moment with the thought that Uncle Kyle, Carole, and now Ginger had stood by my side and defended my case to Principal Halfourd. It knocked me over to think of the kindness shown by my supporters. I gulped, choking down my feelings. I suspected if I started crying, I might never be able to stop.

I stormed to the kitchen and told Hanna I had to see Peggy. She shared her concern that it was too late at night, but, sensing my determination, she looked the other way. With a quick wave, I ran out the front doors of the manor, into the night, and down the gravel road to Peggy's white picket fence. I hadn't seen much of Peggy since my return home. Yet, there she stood under her front porch light, stooped over and waving at me as best she could. I eased the gate open, latched it behind me, and ran into her outstretched arms.

"Oh dear, I'm so glad you've come to visit me. You have some good news," Peggy said.

"It's great to be back to normal … with no supernatural activity."

"Paige, we don't have a lot of time. Carole is coming by, and she needs some help with something for her father. The note from your teacher … what's his name?"

"Mr. Higgins?"

"Yes, isn't it great? You've been given a second chance at Camlachie High. Just take it and don't second-guess it. That's my advice. I wanted to see you and tell you in person how happy I am that you're better. I'm praying that all the negative energy on the estate has been dealt with. You have so many supporters who are working with you, including me and our friends, the spirits from the light, and our guardian angels. Have you heard from Conall or Mackenzie yet?"

"I'm afraid I haven't been very receptive since I've been home."

"Don't trouble yourself. Just finish out your school year. That's all that matters now. And above all, don't forget to do your protection prayers, Paige."

"Well … I can't say that I've been doing them much. My mind is so caught up on what happened at the cottage, on Ariana, and my parents soon to arrive home. Not to mention Grandma's health. I will say them tonight, I promise."

"This time, say the following spiritualists' prayer before you go to sleep."

Dear God:
Please cleanse, clear, fill and encapsulate me
in the white Christ light of healing and protection.
Please remove all negative energies and entities from me
and send them to their proper plane.
Please close the aura against their return,
and in their place put the highest and most powerful vibrations.
Thank you, dear God, our Heavenly Father.

I hugged Peggy's bent-over, fragile body and bid her adieu. I was grateful for her support and much-needed input. Imagine being accepted back at school, not suspended like I thought I would be. I have to admit I was surprised my ancestral gift — my second sight — hadn't somehow revealed the good news to me ahead of time, but I didn't have anything to prove to myself. Mom and Grandpa had the gift of second sight too, maybe even Grandma. Hanna definitely did. I wasn't alone in this.

As I jogged back to the estate, I heard, *Godspeed, Paige*. It was Peggy's blessing, and I was grateful for it. To finally get some exercise was an added bonus on this particular night, as the full moon guided my way home. When I entered the kitchen, Hanna was having tea with my grandparents at the breakfast nook. I slid into my seat next to Hanna, opposite to my grandparents, and joined the hearty conversation. I was over the moon to be home, safe and sound, again. My life had finally returned to normal.

CHAPTER ELEVEN

I kept my promise to attend classes and to finish out the school year. My trusty Volkswagen, Lucille, got me to school on time just as the bell rang each day. I loved my cabriolet convertible and often thought of Dexter, who had taken his time to rebuild her and paint her my favourite colour, metallic royal blue. I missed Dexter — the one who'd supported my family, not the one who'd tried to kill me. He had been possessed, and I wish I had recognized the signs earlier. Maybe I could have helped him survive his ordeal.

"Paige? Paige, snap out of it. Are you participating today or not?" asked Mr. Higgins. "It's your turn to play your composition on the drums. We are waiting, young lady."

I marched to the eight-piece Ludwig drum set arranged at the side of the classroom and noticed a cello, encased bass, an electric guitar, and smaller instruments like a harmonica and flute. I realized I had not heard any of my peers' musical pieces. It made me nervous.

In our household, learning to play the drums was almost a rite of passage, though it was a bit of a chore at times, especially with Dad as my teacher. It was "our thing," what we did together, as we retreated to our Scarborough basement and took out our daily frustrations on Dad's Pearl drum set.

Luckily, my musical skill set came in handy now, as life took its twists and turns. In fact, I had composed a surf rock song years ago, and my classmates were about to hear it for the first time.

Played with the intensity of Ron Wilson's drumming on the original score of the band Surfaris' "Wipe Out," a legendary sixties song Dad loved and had played often, the piece lasted close to five minutes. I was so absorbed in my performance that I was unaware of my peers. When I finished playing, the room was so silent you could hear a pin drop, and then my classmates began to clap, and cheer, and whistle. I guess it was a hit. Note to self: *Share this moment with Dad upon his return.*

Mr. Higgins just stood there for a minute, his mouth hanging open. "Well, P-P-Paige ... you seem to have more musical talent than I thought. Your theory exam went well and now this. I really underestimated you. Sorry about that, kiddo."

"Sorry for ... ?"

"My earlier doubts. You know ... I thought you were a bad ... well, let's just say I didn't think you were too serious about school. Apparently, I was wrong."

I smiled to put him at ease and felt a sense of relief and validation. "No worries, Mr. Higgins. I understand where you're coming from."

Later that day, Carole searched me out after hearing rumours about my conversation with Mr. Higgins. She asked me what was in his note, and I just didn't want to get into it, especially after all that had happened with Ariana. I assumed Carole would be highly suspicious of another new friend suddenly coming to my rescue. I was sure she didn't know who Ginger was. I gave a lame explanation that he was threatening to expel me from class but he came around when he heard me play the drums. I felt terrible lying to Carole — not

Dad joined in on the hug and the three of us clung to each other for a minute, enjoying our private moment together. "We missed you!"

"How was the flight?"

"Oh, you know, fun as always," Dad said with a chuckle. "We don't like those long flights. They're torture to us, sitting there all that time. We're just happy to be back."

"Boy, are we ever!" Mom's eyes sparkled, despite how tired she must have been. "It's so great to be home. And you know your dad, Paige. He wriggled about in his seat and performed deep tissue therapy on his hips. The flight attendants asked him how to do it for their long flights, so your dad kindly showed them. It passed the time." She smiled and gave Dad a fond look. "And I finished my last news article. I'll email it tomorrow. Most of all, we're happy to be home with you. After your unfortunate time at the cottage, you look well. Are you, dear?"

"Oh yeah, I'm over that completely. I had my last checkup and all my blood tests came back normal. Hanna and Grandpa have been looking after me. And I've been helping out with Grandma. We're all good. No need to start the worrying already, Mom."

"You're right, Paige. It's late. I guess we'll navigate our way to the guesthouse. Kevin, can you grab the flashlight from the kitchen drawer?" Mom asked.

A vision popped into my mind as Mom spoke. I saw myself heading for the basement, that same flashlight in my hand. I reached the bottom of the stairs enveloped in darkness, ready to flick on the light, when I saw the eerie amber glow of hellhounds' eyes. I shook the thought right out of my mind.

"No, no. Take my room. I cleaned it up a bit and changed the sheets. I'll sleep in the living room on the sofa. I already told everyone where you'll be staying, and we'll fix up another bedroom for you tomorrow. I'm afraid Allan Brewer, our new landscaper, and his daughter, Trixie, are living in the guesthouse. They had nowhere else to stay."

"Pardon me?" asked Dad. "Who are they?"

"Remember, Allan who looked out for me? Never mind, we can talk about it tomorrow, Dad. No rush."

"You're right; it'll have to wait. I'm beat. C'mon Lori, let's go to bed."

My heart soared as I watched Dad try to carry all the bags to my room, sparing Mom the trouble. I had missed them so much. I would love to have stayed up all night to hear their stories, but they knew I had summer school in the morning. Always the parents. *No rest for the wicked* popped into my head. I shook it off. And on that thought, I nestled into the longest couch ever made, pulled up a cozy duvet, and fell sound asleep.

CHAPTER TWELVE

It was the beginning of July, and the weather couldn't have been more perfect. As each cloudless day rolled by, the sun sparkled, and birds serenaded me from the treetops. A light breeze kept the air refreshing. Unfortunately, summer school was my penance, and as I slipped into Lucille, I was determined to put the past year's events behind me. I had started my journey to re-learn calculus. Math came easily to me, so I wasn't worried about the material we were studying; I was worried that I would be spending too much time away from the estate, away from Grey Owl, Uncle Kyle, and my family and friends who needed me.

As I pulled into the high school's newly paved parking lot, I felt nostalgic for a moment, knowing my time there would soon be at an end. I'd learned many valuable lessons from my teachers and principal at Camlachie High. The understanding and forgiveness they'd afforded me made my heart full.

Amidst the haunting on the O'Brien estate and all the other supernatural activity, it was surreal to be going to summer school; it seemed almost too normal for me. I understood the need to finish, but learning math seemed insignificant at this point, when I knew I should be preparing myself for the spiritual journey ahead. Nevertheless,

I retrieved my keys from the ignition and waltzed into my temporary second home.

Math was held in a cramped classroom located next to the boiler room, which reminded me of a scene from a slasher movie. That, along with the fact that I really hadn't made any friends at my new high school — other than Carole ... and Ginger, sort of — made me a bit anxious. My chest tightened. I held my textbook high and used it as a shield while I pounded on my chest with my other hand — a useful anxiety-busting technique I learned from the nurse at my old high school.

I happened to be a few minutes late, again, and this seemed to disturb Mrs. Jamieson. She ushered me to the last remaining seat in the dimly lit room, a frown on her wrinkly old face. *What in the world is she wearing?* I couldn't help staring at her frilly white dress with a hideous pink bow attached at her waist. It seemed inappropriate somehow, like she was dressed for a luncheon. We began with a review of basic algebra — x and y are called variables, yadda yadda yadda. It took about a minute for my eyes to glaze over and my ears to focus on the tick-tick-ticking of the clock.

A tap on my shoulder startled me. I let out a low yelp, and Mrs. Jamieson shot me a dirty look. Her cat-eye glasses accentuated her bug-eyed glare. I certainly wasn't winning her graces any time soon. I was relieved when she headed back to her desk and I could bury myself in the assignment she'd given us.

"Psst. Paige!"

I stopped working, surprised by the familiar voice whispering to me from behind. I looked around to find Ariana, her black hair tied in a ponytail and a warm smile on her pale, bony face. She was wearing a low-cut red dress, like she was planning to attend a cocktail party after class.

"Hi, Ariana," I whispered. I was so surprised to see her that I almost forgot to return her smile. "What are you doing here?"

"I figured you'd be in this class, so I got late approval and scored the seat behind you, apparently. Sweet."

I heard a soft voice, perhaps trying to warn me in my consciousness, but I paid it no mind as I basked in the warmth of Ariana's joy at seeing me. It made me happy to know she had gone out of her way to be in my class. We would be summer school buddies.

"Fantabulous," I said, much louder than I had intended.

The teacher stopped in the middle of her additional instructions and stared at me.

"Excuse me. Am I interrupting your conversation? Would you like to repeat what you just said to the class?"

"Uh, no," I replied sheepishly. "Sorry."

Ariana and I didn't talk for the rest of the class, but we communicated nonetheless. No words were exchanged, just feelings. Ariana was glad to see me and happy to have an excuse to leave the house more often. She'd been lonely since we parted ways in the hospital and was excited at the prospect of having a new friend. I wasn't sure how I knew this; it wasn't the usual telepathy that allowed me to communicate with Peggy, or Carole, or my other family members. It was more like what I felt in my spirit wolf form; visions and feelings were used more often than language.

After class, Mrs. Jamieson detained me to sign a sheet saying that I had arrived late and to scold me for talking during class. She seemed like a nice enough lady. Probably just at the end of her career, ready to retire and less than thrilled to be teaching remedial classes during the summer. I found Ariana waiting for me as I left the building. She asked if I wanted to walk home together, but I pointed to Lucille and offered her a ride instead.

"You named your car? Wait, you own a car?" she asked, chuckling. "Why don't we go into town for a late lunch? That was a long class. I'm starving! I bet you are too."

My stomach rumbled, but I had promised Hanna I would be home right after class to help her make dinner. She was tired from all the extra work looking after Grandma, and I'd offered to lighten her load. When I explained this to Ariana, she frowned and said she understood, but I knew she was disappointed.

"Okay," I said, though the sick feeling in my gut told me it was a bad decision. "What's the harm? Have you been to Magellan's? They have the best Greek salad in town."

While we drove towards the waterfront, Ariana passed on warm wishes from Sarah, BAPS' mom, and told me that her business was doing quite well, even with her son away at university. Ariana told me she thought Sarah was a really nice lady, though she could be a little too superstitious at times. When I pressed Ariana to elaborate, she simply said Sarah didn't speak too highly of the O'Brien estate. I changed the subject to avoid any conversation about the hauntings that had occurred over the past year. I really wanted our friendship to flourish, and I didn't want to drive Ariana away by talking about earthbounds, angels, or spirit wolves, not to mention hellhounds. *What would she think of me?*

Our salads arrived rather quickly, and much to my delight, Ariana devoured bite after bite.

"I'm really glad you decided to have lunch with me," Ariana said as she laid her fork on the empty plate. "This restaurant is rad. Love the decor with the ocean netting and tropical fish. She sighed and pulled her knees into her chest resting her feet on the bench. "This is wicked, right? It's so good to get to know you better."

I beamed. "You, too. So, what do you like to do for fun? It must be a big change to move to "Hicksville" from "The

6"." When I mentioned *hicksville* my gut felt like it'd been punched. I knew it was wrong to nickname Camlachie in a derogatory way.

"Oh. You like our Toronto treasure, Drake, too? I love his music. Didn't he put Toronto on the map in this big ol' world of ours. Imagine using an area code ... 416 and changing it to "The 6". And yes, it's different. But I'm sure you understand." Ariana strained her eyes for a moment, as if she was looking right through me. "Back home, I spent a lot of time training in Krav Maga. I was just awarded my black belt a few weeks before I moved here."

I had no clue what that was and told her so, feeling a bit naive.

"It's an Israeli martial art. It's widely known as one of the most practical martial arts out there."

"That sounds really intense. What gave you the fighting bug?"

Ariana's eyes refocused on me, but she seemed flustered for a moment. "It's not fighting. It's self-defence. In the world we live in, I think it's crucial to know how to protect yourself."

"I agree." An image of Journey, my spirit wolf, flashed through my mind.

While dropping Ariana off at BAPS' house, my thoughts ran to my ex, Bradley Adam Parkman. Sometimes, it was still difficult to accept the fact that he went away to university and left me alone on the O'Brien estate without any further communication. My heart ached.

"Ariana, I can pick you up for school in the morning," I said, before she exited Lucille.

"Thanks, Paige, but I prefer to walk. It clears my mind for the day, you know, being out in nature and all. But if you want to give me a ride home, I'm down with that."

I smiled politely and nodded as she slammed the car door.

I watched as she marched to the rear of the house. It seemed strange to me that she didn't enter through the front door, but I dismissed the thought. And as I glanced back to watch her round the corner, I noticed a swanky, silver sports car parked beyond the single car garage. *Wait, what? Is that Ariana's car?*

I drove home on autopilot and parked Lucille in the front drive of O'Brien Manor. When I reached over the seat to grab my backpack, I noticed a white feather sitting on top of it. That was curious, indeed.

As I ambled through the elegant entryway, I was overwhelmed by the smell of garlic and roasting meat. My heart sank. I'd lost track of time, and dinner was ready. My cell phone flashed six o'clock. Hanna peeked around the corner into the foyer and gave me a curious look. Her drawn face and pale skin accentuated the gravity of the situation.

"Hanna, I'm so sorry," I said, knowing I was guilty as charged. "I let you down." I dropped my bag and slunk into the kitchen.

"It's okay, Paige. But it's unlike you to not follow through on your promise. I'll forgive you this time." She feigned a smile.

I was thankful to be given the honour of serving my parents — and Hanna and my grandparents, too — a welcome home dinner. We were united once again. I rambled on about class, and when Grandpa asked why I'd come home so late, I lied and said that I was reviewing the material at the school library so I wouldn't fall behind. Though I realized my white lies were mounting, for some reason I was compelled not to mention Ariana any more than I had to. I sensed my family would hit me with a barrage of questions about her and our new friendship, and I was still making my mind up about who she really was.

I directed the conversation at Dad to change the subject. "So tell us about Italy. Are you glad you accepted the locum and helped out that chiropractor? I hope his mom is better now."

Dad nodded at me. "Yes, his mom is much better. Nice of you to ask. But we'd rather hear about you and about Ted and Helen. We don't want to bore you with our stories just yet."

"Now, Kevin, come on," Grandpa said. "We know our sad stories and so do you. Let's hear some good ones. We've been waiting anxiously for your return. There's lots of time to talk about our problems later."

Grandpa smiled and nudged Dad's hand. I found it interesting that Grandpa sat Dad at the head of the table, where he normally took charge.

"Well ... let's see. Which story should we tell first, Lori? The one about the missing spaghetti dish or the pizza story? Or how about the fish story?" Dad laughed.

"Oh my! You go ahead with the fish story, honey," mom replied. "A warning, though: it may make you sick to your stomach." She tossed her head back and laughed in her endearing, carefree way, sending her curly auburn hair across her face.

"Okay, then. You know how when you travel to another country you have your own expectations? As you know, Lori here loves seafood," Dad said as he nodded at Grandpa. Then Dad turned to me. "I took your mom to an exquisite seaside restaurant in Monterosso al Mare. She ordered the seafood platter. Well ... the look on her face ..." Dad laughed, glancing at Mom as he relived the memory. "The fish still had its head, tail, and everything in between, and the platter came with octopus and calamari with no breading, no deep-frying like we're used to here. Your mom could barely look at it, let alone eat it. So I let her have some of my steak while I scarfed down some of her seafood. We didn't want to insult the chef, who we'd been watching all night as he visited each table at the end of the guests' meal. We'll never forget that night, will we, honey?" He studied mom with a loving look in his baby-blue eyes, and I noticed more greying at his temples.

"No, we certainly won't. But what I'd like to remember most is the walk home under a full moon and sparkling stars. Remember their magical reflection in the Mediterranean Sea, hon?" Mom asked rhetorically. "We strolled along arm in arm and stopped at an ice cream stand by the beach ... looking for gelato. Imagine our surprise when they informed us they make the finest homemade ice cream. It was the best we've ever had." It was impossible to miss the softness in Mom's voice or the twinkle in her eyes as she spoke.

"Sounds wonderful," I said, enjoying their tender moment.

After dinner, I helped clear the table and then told every-one I was tired from my first day of school. Of course, this set off my parents' alarms.

"Wait, Paige. We haven't heard much from you. You can't be that tired. How long is your class? Four hours? What did you do after that?" Mom asked, as she joined me in the kitchen. "Poor Hanna waited for your help." Hanna opened her mouth to protest, but Mom cut her off and said, "Don't try to deny it, Hanna. I saw you watching the clock. You were waiting for Paige."

"I lost track of time in the library, that's all." I was desper-ate to change the subject. "So ... which part of the estate will you and Dad be staying in?"

"Grandpa made arrangements with Allan and Trixie for them to move into the cottage. He hired a renovator to fix it up, so it's livable now. And we're moving into the guesthouse in a few days, after all of the cleanup is done."

"Paige, with everything you've been through, I didn't want to bother you with the details of where your parents would be living. You're more than welcome to stay with us in the manor, if your parents don't mind, that is," Grandpa said, as he placed a glass on the kitchen countertop.

"Mom, maybe we should discuss this later. And that's fine, grandpa. No harm done. Wait. What cleanup?"

"It's a mess, Paige. I don't know who those people are or what they did in our family home, but there was dirt and leaves, and some of the furniture was overturned and partially ruined. Dad will have to replace some of the dining room chairs. And our bedroom—"

"What about your bedroom?"

"It has ... let's just say it has a musty smell like ... animals. Who are Allan and Trixie anyways?"

"They're my friends, Mom. Who knows what happened? Maybe some animals broke in and caused the mess. If it wasn't for Allan and his stepdaughter, I don't know what I would've done these last six months. Dad mentioned Allan once on the phone."

"Okay, okay. Easy now. Perhaps I do remember mention of Allan. I'm sorry to accuse your friends. We're good and you need some rest. We'll talk about this again tomorrow, okay?" Mom gave me that understanding smile that always made me feel guilty.

That night as I lay in bed, I felt ashamed for lying to my family, and I wasn't sure why I was doing it so often lately. I fell asleep with an uneasy feeling, dreading the consequences of my deceitfulness. In my heart I knew it would catch up with me eventually; things like that always did.

CHAPTER THIRTEEN

Calculus class was over for the week, and it was finally the weekend. We had been reviewing limits, a topic I'd always found rather dull, but I'd become engrossed in the lesson. As much as Mrs. Jamieson came across as a grumpy old lady, she was an excellent teacher. With some reluctance, I realized I was actually interested in math for the first time in years. Her lesson plans were always well thought out. She would introduce a topic, give us a practical example of how to use it in the real world, and then walk us through sample problems we might see on the exam. We were learning math by doing rather than by memorizing formulae.

After class, Ariana and I walked out to Lucille together. Ariana had apparently been learning calculus with an after-school tutor since she was thirteen, so the class was far too simple for her.

"I can't stand learning the same things over and over again," she lamented. "I wish we would move on to more complicated stuff."

I didn't respond, but I wondered what she was doing in summer school if she'd already learned all the material. I smiled at her and changed the subject.

"So, what have you been doing in your free time? Are there any Krav Maga classes around here?"

Ariana gave me an anticipatory smile. "Well, actually, I was going to ask you if you wanted me to teach you some moves."

"Well, I … I really need to get home today," I said. "My mom was pretty upset about the other day. I was supposed to help Hanna with dinner."

"We won't be long, I promise!" Ariana placed her hand on my arm and gave me a heartfelt smile.

I rolled my eyes and gave in. Ariana was desperate for a friend, and I knew I couldn't let her down. Mom would have to understand somehow.

"Okay, but just an hour. Then I have to step on it and get home. Where do you want to do this?"

"You know the woods just beyond Sarah's house where I'm staying? There's a nice big clearing."

We drove to the woods around the corner from the estate. I was worried we would run into my parents or Allan on a stroll, but no one was around. I hated having secrets from my family, but my instincts confirmed I needed to keep this one to myself.

"Okay, we're going to start with something pretty basic and practical," Ariana explained as she set her backpack down on the grass. She drew a rather large knife from her bag. The four inch blade was serrated on one side, and the hilt had a ruby set in it.

"Whoa!" I whispered. "What's with the knife?"

"A lot of Krav Maga is learning to defend yourself against attackers." She stood up and positioned herself in front of me with her left leg forward and her right leg slightly bent, knife in hand. "I'm going to strike downward at your left shoulder. You're going to bring your left arm up at a 90-degree angle and deflect my blow. At the same time, you're going to punch me in the jaw with your right fist. Then, drive my right arm back and knee me in the chest."

"Uh, that's a lot to take in," I said, hesitant but curious. Then I thought, *Why not?* and decided to chance it.

It took me several tries to really understand what Ariana was attempting to teach me, but eventually I deflected the knife blow like she had instructed. It was kind of empowering. I felt stronger and more agile with each attempt. On my last power move, I drove my knee into Ariana's chest with such force that she toppled over onto the grass and her knife went flying.

"Oh, Ariana, I'm so sorry!" I squealed and ran over to help her up.

She raised her arm, righted herself with alarming speed, and laughed. "No problem, Paige. You're doing really well! It almost feels like you've taken some sort of martial arts before."

"Nope. You're just a really good teacher, Ariana." I spied the knife, sauntered over and picked it up. When I touched the hilt, it was so hot I dropped it. Wincing from the pain, I noticed that the palm of my hand had turned bright red.

"What happened, Paige?" Ariana asked as she approached and reached out for my hand.

I withdrew it and rubbed my palms together. "Nothing. I'm fine."

Ariana sat down and motioned for me to join her. She opened her backpack and tossed a few items onto the ground beside her. Balling up my fist to hide my burn, I bent my knees and slumped next to her. Ariana began arranging six candles in a tight circle equidistant between us. She placed what looked like an old drinking goblet in the middle of the circle and held her left palm over it. With her other hand, she picked up the knife and then looked up at me.

"Do you believe in witchcraft, Paige?" she asked suddenly.

I was taken aback. "Uh ... y-you mean like, magic?"

"Some might call it that, yes. But it's not like in the movies."

I wasn't sure how to respond, so I said nothing. Ariana didn't offer any further explanation either. Instead, she set the knife down and lit the candles with a mini-lighter. She muttered something, and the air around me became icy cold. She handed me the knife.

"Take it, Paige."

Reluctantly, I reached out for the hilt. I was relieved that it felt cool to the touch this time. I heard a whisper of voices in the recesses of my mind, much like I'd experienced in the hospital and since then, but I couldn't make out what they were saying. I shook it off.

"Run the blade along my palm, then yours," she said calmly. "The blood will fall into the chalice. Then we will join our blood together and be bonded forever."

A fierce shiver ran down my spine. "What ... what do you mean?"

"It's a sacrificial rite, a sacred bond between friends. It binds our souls. You know, like blood sisters."

I threw the knife down in front of me, knocking over one of the candles, which instantly blew out. The air temperature returned to normal, and the voices in the back of my head receded. I stood up and grabbed my backpack.

"I'm sorry, Ariana. I'm not comfortable with this. And I faint at the sight of blood. I guess ... I'll see you tomorrow."

I ran back to my car wiping tears away as I went not wanting to hear Ariana's reply. I realized I didn't know Ariana at all; she was clearly into something twisted. My friends were right. I drove to the estate, and raced into the manor. I really needed to see a friendly face.

Mom stood in the kitchen, drinking juice from a chalice. I shivered at the sight of it. She greeted me with wide eyes; I must have seemed flustered as I approached her.

"What's wrong, sweetie?" she asked, and proceeded to give me a big hug.

I rested my head on her shoulder and sighed. "I just had a rough day." I wanted to tell mom about Ariana, but the words wouldn't come. It was probably for the best anyway; there was no point dwelling on Ariana now. I looked up to Above for a brief moment, and pleaded, *No more complications, please. Don't I have enough already?*

"Maybe it will help you to share it with me. I am your mom. I know I haven't been here for you lately, especially after the cottage fiasco, but I'm here now. Let me in, Paige. Don't push me away. I can see something's troubling you, dear."

"Mom, we have better things to talk about, honestly. It's summer school stuff. How's Grandma today?" I asked, hoping my manoeuvre thwarted any further questioning.

"She's been moving around the manor without her walker. It's her first day. But she's tired now. She's lying down in her room. You can go and see her if you like." Mom tipped her head toward Grandma's bedroom. "She can hear us," she whispered. "Go."

I marched down the hallway and, sure enough, found Grandma standing near the doorway. She surprised me with a bear hug.

"Aha! I've got you," she said, smiling. "Look, I'm walking, Paige." Grandma strutted around the room and looked as good as new.

"Fantastic, Grandma. Now we're all healed."

As soon as I said it, I remembered Grey Owl's warning to heal myself by the babbling brook. I thought, *That's it! I can shake off whatever witchy witchcraft Ariana tried to use on me by touching the healing rock.* And with this lightbulb moment, I heard, *Before you do that, come and see me, Paige. We need to discuss something. Now. Make an excuse.*

Startled, I turned to Grandma and said, "I've got to go. I'll be back shortly."

I was out the door before Grandma could reply. I avoided the kitchen when I heard the clanging noise of pots and pans. Mom and Hanna were cooking and I was guilty by absentia once again. The only voice that would command me to *come now* was Peggy's. She only did that when I was in danger, and I wondered if this had anything to do with Ariana.

I ran down the gravel road and jumped over the white picket fence, impressed by my athleticism. Sometimes I had to keep my mind occupied with trivial achievements such as this when trouble brewed. The heavy, red storm door had been replaced with a Victorian-style kitchen screen door. It was quite pretty. I eased it open and called Peggy's name, but there was no response. I thought it was unusual, but it was not the first time for this to happen. I felt a pit in my stomach, remembering the day I found her unconscious in a snow bank. Shaking the memory off, I entered the communications room ... probably the only room in the world devoid of technology. Instead, it was a safe haven for spirit communication. Still no sign of Peggy—no tea cup, no book on the end table. Upon entering the kitchen, I noticed the steam from the tea kettle and ensured the burner was turned off. Check, it was. I trudged out the side door, and as I headed along the path leading to the backyard, I bumped right into Carole.

"Surprise!" she said with a chuckle. "Figures only Peggy could get through to you. I've been trying to send you telepathic messages to meet up, but got nothing. There you go, Peggy," she yelled over her shoulder. "You were right. She's only on your frequency these days." Carole laughed and hit my arm. "Wait, is something wrong?"

"No, no. It's just so good to see you," I replied, hugging her for a moment. "Let's see what Peggy wants."

I turned the corner and was delighted to find Peggy seated at a bronze, ornately carved bistro table. Peggy's favourite teapot, the orange floral one, was strategically placed in the middle with three cups. I thought, *Who will have the honour of pouring the tea this time.*

"Paige. So happy you could steal away for a bit. Don't you know Carole and I miss you?" Peggy asked. Her blazing blue eyes melted my heart. I felt a pang of loneliness and realized how much I missed my friends.

"Sorry. With summer school, my parents returning, and Grandma's problem, I've been distracted. I should have just come over to see you at some point."

"No apology necessary between friends, child. We miss you, don't we, Carole?"

"For sure! You've been incommunicado. We're worried, that's all."

"Well, I'm here now," I said, my eyebrows rose as I searched Peggy's eyes.

Peggy gracefully poured the tea. "It seems all I get these days are warnings for you. Have a sip of tea, Paige," Peggy said with a hint of concern. "Relax, dear."

I slurped the delicious tea. It was my favourite green tea with jasmine that Mom had introduced me to on one of our few shopping escapades. I took a breath and cleared my mind.

Finally, now I can read you. Are you distressed? Carole asked.

No, not really.

She shot me a quizzical look.

"Paige, there is a dark, shadowy figure in your aura. Nothing to be too alarmed about right now, but it could progress into a bigger problem. I cannot see the face of this darkness, but she is hiding who she really is from you. I think we've narrowed it down. Carole reminded me of your new friend that you met in the hospital, yes?"

I nodded and squirmed in my chair. I didn't want to offer any information about Ariana just yet.

"I can't say for sure, but it might be her. Is her name Annie, by chance?" Peggy asked.

When I opened by mouth to reply, stomach pains overcame me, and I crouched over in agony. I fought to keep from throwing up. I wasn't sure I could make it home, but I had to get out of there. "I've got to leave now. My stomach is killing me. Must've been something I ate today."

"Oh no. Maybe I have something in my remedies cabinet to calm your stomach," Peggy said.

I shook my head and mumbled an apology as I slid from my chair and stumbled down the path. As I rounded the corner of Peggy's house, I stopped for a moment to gather myself. I clutched my stomach as I trotted along the gravel road, and as soon as I reached the O'Brien estate, the pain stopped. I heard Mackenzie's voice: *Beware, Paige. Ariana's strength is increasing. She practices black magic.*

My thoughts raced that night as I lay in bed trying to make sense of Ariana and her introduction to Witchcraft 101. And then my thoughts shifted to the events while snowbound at the dilapidated cottage. *What have I gotten my friends into?* My memory was vague, and I tried to get the image of the demon out of my mind. Had it been after me, or Allan, that day? It was hard to believe that such a creature had made contact and even more surprising was the fact I could see it.

I tried to fall asleep, but the warning from Peggy popped into my mind. What did she mean? Why was I in danger? I knew something was brewing on the estate, once again, but I had no idea what it could be, and it didn't seem like anyone else did either. I hadn't heard messages from anyone other than Peggy and Mackenzie, and I couldn't figure out why. There was no communication from Conall or Uncle Kyle. Even Grey Owl was distant. Perhaps I was overtired. Peggy had warned me not to communicate telepathically with anyone when I experienced fatigue.

My cell phone vibrated and as I reached for it, I knocked it off the side of my bed reminding me how clumsy I can be. As it buzzed around on the hardwood floor, I read a text from Ariana.

Sorry for today, Paige. I saw the friendship ritual on some website, thought it would be fun. I didn't mean to freak you out. I know I'm a little intense ... guess that's why I've never had any real friends. I thought we were becoming friends, guess I screwed things up again. I'm skipping calculus tomorrow. See you.

I swallowed hard to clear the lump from my throat. Maybe I had misjudged the situation. Maybe Ariana was just trying to solidify our friendship, albeit in a strange way. It was pretty late, so I let the text go unanswered. I needed time to figure out what Ariana's intentions were and whether or not she was someone I could trust. I felt a pain in my gut again, but this time it was the nagging kind, the kind you get when you try to talk yourself into something that's not quite right. The warnings I'd received from Peggy, Uncle Kyle, and Mackenzie should have been enough to tell me otherwise.

CHAPTER FOURTEEN

Ariana was true to her word; she did not attend class the next morning. The desk behind me was left vacant, and I missed the sounds of Ariana fidgeting in her seat. As much as I tried to focus on the lesson Mrs. Jamieson was teaching, I could not stop thinking about Ariana. Her fascination with witchcraft freaked me out, but it seemed like she was just a misunderstood, quirky girl, much like me. I wish I had more guidance on the issue, but it seemed like every time I wanted to talk to Mom about it, the words would not come together. As thoughts raced around in my head, I found myself slumping back in my chair. My eyes fluttered until I dozed off.

Standing still in the thick forest beyond the estate, I observed errant rays of sunshine penetrating the towering trees surrounding me, creating intricate webs of light. I danced around the rays, singing and laughing. My body vibrated and I felt more alive than usual. My extremities tingled, and my skin felt soothingly warm to the touch. Then, as if someone took a black marker and painted dark clouds above me, the temperature dropped drastically and I shuddered. I was so cold my teeth chattered, and I hugged myself in the hopes of warming up but instead continued to shiver. Startled by the sound of rustling leaves, I jerked around to find a large, black figure loitering in the shrubs, its floating red eyes watching me. I shrieked and darted off in the opposite direction.

Sharp branches stabbed at my arms and legs as I charged through the woods, I smacked right into a thick, low limb and nearly lost my footing, but I pushed on, determined not to cry. Glancing over my shoulder, I could not spy my stalker and hoped it had been a hallucination.

"It's still here," whispered a familiar voice.

I reeled around. It was Trixie. She was curled up in a ball beside an expanse of bushes. Her face and shoulders were bloodied, and dark red tears fell from the corners of her eyes.

"Trixie! What happened? Are you okay? What's going on?"

"She's coming for us, Paige. You let her in, and now she's coming for us."

As much as I wanted to hug and protect Trixie, my own fear overwhelmed me. I stood paralyzed and was so cold that I was surely at risk of frostbite. I fought through it and managed to approach Trixie. She screamed so loud that I thought my eardrums would burst. I covered my ears with my palms and knelt down against a tree. I tried to call out her name, but my voice failed me.

Footsteps sounded behind me. Someone approached. Trixie's piercing scream was so loud that it seemed to blur my vision. I wanted to run to her, to comfort her, but I was frozen in place. I couldn't understand how I heard the footsteps over Trixie's screams, but they continued to sound closer. Time moved at a glacial pace. Eventually, I saw a figure emerge in my periphery, taking careful, calculated steps towards Trixie. The figure was clearly human but had a strange, shapeless appearance, like it was a caricature of a person or maybe an anime character that had been badly drawn. The figure lashed out at Trixie with superhuman speed. It grabbed her by the throat, lifting her into the *air as if she were weightless. Trixie's screams subsided. I watched in horror as the figure lifted a knife and drove the blade into Trixie's chest.*

"Trixie!" I cried out, jerked back to reality as my body hit the cold floor beneath my desk. I could feel all the eyes in the room pressing against me.

"Paige!" screamed Mrs. Jamieson. "What the devil are you doing?"

What the devil ... Exactly! I got to my feet, brushed myself off, and collected my belongings. "I'm sorry, I have to go."

Without waiting for a response, I fled from the room and tore down the hallway, jumped into Lucille, and raced home to the estate. I could have just called Allan, but I was afraid he would confirm my suspicions — that this dream wasn't a dream at all. When I reached the end of our long, cobblestone driveway, Allan waited for me, pacing outside the manor doorway as if he'd been expecting me. His stooped shoulders and pained expression set off sirens for me.

"Allan, did something bad happen to Trixie?" I shouted, as I slammed my car door.

"We're not sure what's wrong with her," he answered, his voice cracking. "We were having lunch with your parents, and she just fell over in her chair like someone had punched her. She screamed and then started convulsing. She's resting on the couch now. I wasn't sure if I should call for an ambulance or not."

I gave Allan a tight hug. "How is she doing now? Is she awake?"

"She's asleep, I think. Hanna took her blood pressure, and her heart rate was normal. I don't want to wake her. I think she needs to rest." Allan pushed away from me. "She said something before she collapsed. She said 'Paige, no!' What did she mean, Paige?"

I frowned. "Are you ... do you think I did this to her? I had a dream about Trixie. We were in the forest. Something attacked her."

"It seems like something's up with you lately, Paige. It's like you're hiding something. I ran into Carole yesterday, and she told me both she and Peggy have been trying to warn you about something but you're not listening. I don't know what's going on, but if you know anything that could help Trixie, I need you to tell me. Now."

"I ... uh, there's nothing going on!"

I stormed past Allan and entered the manor to check on Trixie. Hanna leaned against the kitchen doorframe, and gave me a subtle frown when I came into view. I ignored her and rushed into the living room. Trixie lay listless on the couch. Carole stood over her, holding a cold cloth on her forehead.

"Is she okay, Carole?" I whispered.

Trixie rolled over on the couch as her eyes fluttered open.

"She seems okay." Carole absent-mindedly set the cloth in her lap and turned to me. "Paige, I think you need to stop seeing this Ariana girl. Both Peggy and I have had dreams about a girl who is going to spread darkness in your life, like a virus, through you to all of us. Please, Paige, for all of our sakes. I'm begging you to end this friendship before it ruins us ... all."

CHAPTER FIFTEEN

When I reached the cedar trees that lined the path to Bradley's house, I hesitated before stepping onto the property. What was I going to say to Ariana? I couldn't just come out and accuse her of harming Trixie — what if I was wrong? I still felt Ariana was just a misunderstood new friend who was perhaps a little eccentric. But I trusted my faithful friends, and if they felt she was a threat, I needed to figure it out for myself and deal with her. With this new confidence in mind, I approached my ex-boyfriend's house and found the front door ajar. I snuck inside.

Blinking my eyes to adjust to the dimly lit room, I was unable to process the images in my view. It took my pupils a few moments to adjust, and I was horrified to discover Ariana hovering in the middle of the room, swaying back and forth. She was encircled by the largest candles I had ever seen, some just shy of four feet tall. The flickering flame provided the only light in the room; all of the windows had been blackened. To my left was an end table covered in a red tablecloth. It supported a black sphere that gave off a faint red glow and made strange sounds, almost as if it were chanting. Shadows danced around the room, scurrying from one corner to the next. When Ariana finally noticed my presence, she turned to me. Her steely eyes darted back and forth, dark, bottom-less pools set in transparent skin. Her lips, painted a bright blood-red, were curled in an ugly sneer. She bellowed a few words. At first I thought they were directed at me, but they were foreign to my ears. She held the knife with the ruby-set hilt in her right hand.

Finally, she spoke to me. "So nice to see you again, Paige!" She cackled in a shrill, piercing voice.

I'd heard those exact words before, spoken through the lips of Hanna. *So nice to see you again.* A chill ran up my spine and spread goosebumps over my entire body.

"You're just in time to meet my secret weapon. Behold, Beelzebub!" Ariana flung her arms out to her sides and twirled around, pointing aimlessly as she went.

A swarm of flies appeared from each corner, meeting in a vortex in front of me. The flies swirled around, slowly materializing into a dark figure. Red eyes returned my scrutiny, and I watched as wings formed on a dinosaur-like body that transformed into a red dragon. I winced at the foul sulphur smell of the hulking winged beast before me. Beelzebub flew at me and smacked me with his talons, sending me reeling across the floor. The shadows that danced around the room began to take shape—large, ever-changing, dark, translucent bodies with piercing eyes. I knew at once that they must be demons.

Beelzebub hissed as he hovered above me. He raised his wings, exposing four inch-long talons emerging from his feet. An unseen force lifted me into the air, and I found myself floating in front of Beelzebub, shaking, terrified. He studied me with a calculated gaze.

"I am the Prince of Demons, the Lord of the Flies," he bellowed, his tone so sharp that it echoed around me. "I have come for your soul. Come with me, oh Chosen One. Join my forces. Together, we will be unstoppable; we will rule the mortal realm."

I gasped at the sight of him. "I have no idea what you're talking about. Know this: I will never join you!" I tried to sound confident, yet I trembled with fear.

"You speak as if you have a choice. Come with me now, or you will die, and I will claim your soul."

"Then you'll have to kill me!" I shouted. "I will never work for the forces of evil!"

Beelzebub lunged at me with a bloodthirsty glare. Just as he was about to devour me, an orb with a solid center appeared beside me. Beelzebub shrieked and flew backwards, disappearing into a cloud of flies and vanishing through the wall. The white orb took form; it was Archangel Michael, my saviour, with his lengthy sword and shield in hand. Ariana shrieked. She picked up the mammoth diary and flipped to a page, shouting something in a foreign language to Archangel Michael. He seemed frozen in place. She cackled and continued shouting words until her diary slammed shut and lifted itself out of her hands. When Ariana finished her incantation, a ball of energy erupted from her body, tossing both Archangel Michael and me from the house.

I landed on the grass with a thud. As I shook my head to clear my vision, the house disappeared into thin air right before my eyes, just as the demon Beelzebub had. The grass appeared undisturbed, as if it had never held the weight of a home. Left feeling shaken, all I could do was stare at the empty space in front of me. I sensed Archangel Michael beside me, watching me, but I could not work up the energy to acknowledge him just yet.

"Paige, don't let illusions fool you. You know you are the Chosen One, handpicked to fight the evil on the O'Brien estate after all these centuries. And to fight for humankind. It is your destiny, my child."

I knew Archangel Michael was trying to tap into my reasoning mind, but after what I had just witnessed, I doubted my ability to reason at all. In fact, I no longer trusted myself to know what was real and what was not.

He continued. "You come from a long line of spiritual warriors who have always fought against the forces of evil. The spiritual power within you ... the darkness seeks to corrupt it and control you. You're the biggest threat to the realm of demons, but you're also their strongest weapon—if they can get their hands on you."

"What is so important about my family, my ancestry, Archangel Michael? Please tell me. I need you to explain it to me. What's happening to me?"

"Your family is the keeper of the original Seal of Solomon, the ring that our Creator entrusted to King Solomon through me, all those centuries ago. King Solomon was known in his time as a powerful magician and prophet. He grew tired of watching demons hurt his people, so he petitioned to God for help. The Seal allowed him, a mortal, to imprison demons and use them for his own purposes to help build his temple. Unfortunately, with great power comes great temptation. King Solomon succumbed; after all, he was only mortal. That's the danger of powerful magic falling into the wrong hands. Ariana wants the Seal in order to imprison Beelzebub and control his legion of demons for her own purposes. Beelzebub, however, has followed this girl only to gain access to you. He's the one in control and he is manipulating her."

Archangel Michael paused, allowing me to process the facts about King Solomon and my O'Brien ancestry. I swallowed hard and gazed up at him.

"You mean all of this is over some Seal created centuries ago? This is a living nightmare. Do you think my grandpa has known about this all along, that this is the trouble I am to fight? How can that be?" I rose to my feet, bewildered.

"Your grandfather has forgotten your family has the Seal. He had to bury this secret deep within the recesses of his mind, Paige. Understand, the Seal is one of the most sought-after amulets of all time and has been passed down through your ancestry. Humankind believes it is stored in a vault in Italy, but your family is empowered by God Himself to take charge of the very ring He Himself blessed for Solomon. Ariana is seeking clues to its location using the book she inherited from her mother. She told you it was her diary, but it's actually an ancient grimoire, a book of magical spells from centuries ago, granting access to spirits, demons, and angels—all the supernatural entities. She thinks it's the original grimoire, the one handwritten by King Solomon himself. His incantations for summoning demons are the most powerful in the world. And he was the only one who knew Beelzebub by his real name—Beelzebul. King Solomon also practiced exorcisms on those possessed by demons. The grimoire, known as *The Testament of Solomon*, was buried in King Solomon's tomb as he instructed his son, Rehoboam, to do. But later, Rehoboam recovered the book. For what purpose, we do not know. Apparently, Ariana's mother found a version written after Solomon's death, a replica, but it lacks the most powerful of spells. Thankfully, without the original Testament and Seal, Ariana lacks the power to control the demons she has managed to summon using her mother's grimoire. Paige, the Seal represents superhuman wisdom and rule by divine grace. It's the most powerful magical ring in the world. Have you ever wondered why the hellhounds are on your side? They are protecting something; don't you agree?"

I nodded and said, "What happens if Ariana gets the Testament and the Seal?"

Archangel Michael appeared distraught as his wings bristled, puffed up, and widened at his sides. "If the Seal of

Solomon falls into her hands, she will throw your world and, ultimately, the universe into chaos. The hexagram symbolizes the harmony of opposites, a connection between Heaven and Earth. The darkness within her heart will cause perversion, and evil will flood the earthly plane like never before. And combined with Solomon's grimoire, his Testament, she'll control the legions of hell by commanding demons. If humankind does not fight back against this darkness, if they don't learn to control their fears and abolish them, rise above them, they may not be able to reverse the darkness. In Turkey, Italian archaeologists already believe they've found the gate to hell itself. This is the most important battle in the earth's history, fighting against all that is evil."

"Why would Beelzebub ... Beelzebul, whatever, join up with Ariana? I don't understand."

"He lets her think she's in control, but he's manipulating her, using her as a conduit for his energy. With no mortal body, he lacks the power to overcome such a powerful spiritual force as yourself. But through Ariana, using her mortal body and energy, he can attack you physically as well as mentally. If he can defeat you and claim your soul, he can fight back against Heaven and take over the mortal realm." Archangel Michael moved closer and as he did, his wings fluttered and he almost knocked me down. His energy was extreme.

"Please don't come so close to me," I begged. "It's hurting me."

"Sorry, I often forget that your power, though strong, is in human form." He backed off.

I regained my composure. "Well, I've handled what's been thrown at me so far. Let's see ... there's the haunting by Conall, who wanted to kill my entire family, and the haunting by Bradford, who is blaming all of us for something in our past and wants us dead. Dexter, our loyal friend, who

I trusted like my own family, who eventually became possessed by a demon, I assume, and tried to kill me. Oh and let's not forget my most recent fun trapped at the cottage. And seeing that demon. I still wonder if that was an act of God, for me to learn a mortal lesson of some sort. Do you know what, exactly?"

"That … you must decipher for yourself. I cannot interfere with your journey, Paige, but I can help you to fight these demons upon request—by God or by you. Come, let's meet with Gabriel and Archangel Raphael. They will be able to assist you further regarding the Seal."

"Did God sanction this?" At the time, I didn't understand what I was asking.

"Of course He sanctioned this, Paige. It is your destiny."

"So what do I have to do?" I asked, saluting Archangel Michael. It seemed a cheesy response, but I had to maintain my sense of humour throughout this otherworldly time. And it was one human characteristic for which I knew I'd be forgiven.

Archangel Michael paused and studied my face, reminding me once again how powerful his energy was. It almost knocked me over. After a moment's silence, he said, "This is not for me to suggest. I am sanctioned to be one of your protectors. Come, we must seek counsel."

CHAPTER SIXTEEN

My soul hesitated as it reached the ceiling of my bedroom, gazing back at my physical body lying listlessly on the bed. This was not my first out-of-body experience, but it felt strange to me each and every time. However, I was encouraged to move along in spirit with Archangel Michael as my guide, as he carried me up into the heavens to a familiar white room. There, we were joined by Archangel Raphael and a third angel I did not recognize, though I assumed he was Gabriel. He was dressed in a blue gown with matching blue armour that, from the sagging of his shoulders, I guessed was made of some heavy metal. Gabriel spoke telepathically to me.

Paige, I am Gabriel, the Messenger of God, and He has commanded me to help you with this supernatural battle that will take place in the mortal realm. You have met Beelzebul, his original name mentioned in the Testament of Solomon. He is often referred to as the prince of demons. While many refer to him as Beelzebub, most know him as the devil, and he lays claim to being one of the leading heavenly angels known as Lucifer. King Solomon wrote specifically about him in the Testament of Solomon. Beware: he can possess or shapeshift into anyone. He was originally one of us. He was God's greatest creation ... until his ego took hold and he manipulated one third of the angels to fall with him in the hopes that one day they would try to rise up against God, His angels, and anyone caught in between. You, my child, are caught in this battle. It is the ultimate war between good and evil forces. And for that, we need your help.

You are the key to fighting against the most dangerous threat to humankind—the devil that has brought this battle into the mortal realm. Now, humans are awakening to the dark energy invading their consciousness here on Earth. Can you feel the darkness growing, Paige? Typhoons and drought are devastating the world, war is waging in the name of religion, and climate changes have confused people and wildlife. From now on, you will know what to do instinctively, because God is guiding you, Paige, as are we, His soldiers. Trust your instincts, your inner guiding voice. Listen to it. Sometimes the signs will be cryptic, and sometimes they will be obvious, but you must be aware of them. It is the key to your family's welfare.

When Beelzebul sets his demons upon people, it affects those who are angry, frustrated, feeling isolated and alone, insecure, and lost. He commands his demons to enter their bodies and take hold, making them do his bidding in the flesh. With this hidden secret on his side, humanity has no power to fight back until they realize what's happening and take this threat seriously. This war has been waged since the beginning of time. You must awaken those around you to the demons trying to control your lives and make you a part of their team. Evil will befall those closest to you unless you warn everyone. Remember, Paige, the only way to fight evil and its darkness is to shine your light on it, have good thoughts, and live from a place of love. It is human nature to over-analyse, manipulate circumstances, highlight wrongdoing, and pass judgment, thereby feeding fear. Fight it. Turn it around and feed the love. Work towards solutions, positive ones, nurturing an understanding heart capable of forgiveness. Never wallow in self-pity; it is a sin. We know this path can be lonely, *isolating, but realizing your soul's destiny is an essential path to God, to inner peace and joy. When you return to your body, you will know what to do. We thank you, Paige. You are the brave one, our Chosen One.*

***

Bam! I awoke in my body, exactly where I had left it. My brain felt groggy at first, and I clamoured to my feet to gaze out my bedroom window. It was early morning and the birds hadn't begun to chirp yet. I was tiring of the wee hours of the morning. It seemed to be my normal lately, and I scratched my head wondering what had happened to me during the night. Try as I might, I could not remember anything from my elusive dreams.

A pebble crashed against my window followed by another. I looked down, and with a nervous twitch, I pulled on my curls trying to straighten them. Grey Owl motioned for me to join him. I threw on shorts and a T-shirt and ran to meet him in the garden. Grey Owl was huddled with Uncle Kyle in a serious conversation. I was curious and wondered what was so important for them to visit me so early.

"Paige, Grey Owl had a vision of you and the Archangels. But you also met the Angel Gabriel, the one who is the messenger for God. Do you remember anything about this?" Uncle Kyle asked in a concerned tone. His dilated pupils tipped me off that this was going to be a very intense conversation.

"Nope. I can't remember anything. Not a thing. What happened in your vision, Grey Owl, if I may ask?"

"I sensed it was a meeting about the evil closing in on the O'Brien estate and all who live here. Do you remember what they said to you, Paige? It's important. I only saw who was involved; I did not hear the conversation." Grey Owl shifted the weight of his muscular body onto his left leg and as he did, his fringed jacket shook.

"I'm sure it will come to me in time. What has you so upset?"

"When I woke up this morning, I felt compelled to take a stroll through the forest near my home. I found a dead frog, a dead raven, and then a deer. Three deaths in a row ... it's bad luck and means there will be more deaths to follow. It might be birds, animals, or ... humans. I have never encountered this feeling before. I feel ... fear." Grey Owl paused for a moment, taking in a deep breath. "That's when I charged over to Kyle's and here we are."

I was speechless and motioned to my protectors to follow me to the rose garden, where we settled on a bench we'd placed there in Dexter's memory. I called it the Dexter bench. For a brief moment, I felt Dexter's energy — a mighty, compelling force. And I heard a whisper.

It's me, the Inquisitor. I'm here with you when you need me, Paige. God has sanctioned it. Just call my name.

I smiled at Dexter's use of the nickname I had given him for being so nosy about my life and thankful it was helpful in the verification of his spirit in the afterlife. I raised my eyebrows at Grey Owl and Uncle Kyle as I sent my friends the telepathic message I received from Dexter.

Uncle Kyle replied, *Very good, Paige. Always have spirits confirm their identity.*

He winked at me and got to his feet. "I have to return to my reserve. I have an elders meeting. Grey Owl, will you be attending with me?" Uncle Kyle raised his eyebrows, and I noticed how brightly his brown eyes reflected his inner light.

"No, but I thank you, my friend. I need to investigate what's happening a bit further. Paige, I'll be by the brook contacting our ancestors for help. They may show me some visions to aid us in our quest." As he trudged away, a jingling from his belt buckle resounded.

I nodded at Grey Owl and watched as my two protectors left in opposite directions. *When did the change occur? I wondered. When had it become my normal to be masterminding a solution for the oncoming supernatural battle on the O'Brien estate ... and with the help of these spiritually charged humans?* I shivered as I caught a chill, and suddenly I pictured Ariana hovering in mid-air. Startled at the vision, I shook it off and entered the estate through the rickety kitchen screen door. I spied Hanna talking to someone.

"Surprise!" she said as I tiptoed into the room.

Perplexed, I scanned the room searching for my surprise. Out of the shadows waltzed Ariana.

"So nice to see you again, Paige," she said in a determined, guttural voice. I shuddered as I heard each formidable word spoken, knowing I had heard them one too many times before. "I've missed you, my friend. What have you been up to?" Ariana wiggled her eyebrows as she spoke.

"Nothing much," I replied. "I didn't think I'd ever see you again. You just ... disappeared. Into thin air, as a matter of fact." I stared her down as I spoke to her, confident and unafraid. I was tired of her bullying me, trying to intimidate and scare me. *When exactly did my fear turn into a knowing that I would not let Ariana bully me any more?* I couldn't put my finger on it.

Grandma entered the room in her oversized paisley robe and slippers. "I heard a knock at the door. It's so early. Well, it looks like you two need to have a discussion. Come along, Hanna, let's give them some privacy."

Hanna hesitated and asked, "Paige, is everything okay? Do you want me to stay?"

"No, but thanks, Hanna. I've got this." I forced a smile as Hanna and Grandma left the kitchen, chatting as though nothing bad was going down. My grandma's slight build contrasted Hanna's stodgier frame and I was thankful they were fast friends; two of a kind.

"Ariana, what happened to Sarah's house? Where'd it go?" I demanded

"Oh, that." She swung her hips from side to side and sang, "I put a spell on you ... because you're mine."

She continued to hum the song, and as she did, I remembered the day Mom downloaded Annie Lennox's version of it. It was one of her best performances ever. Listening and watching Ariana sing it was creepy.

"Haven't you heard of a little thing called glamouring? Ha ha. Fooled you, did I? Good to know. I must be more powerful than I realized." Her Cheshire cat smile and haunted, empty eyes reflected her dark soul.

"Nope. I've never heard of glamouring. What is it?" I asked, unsure if I wanted to open the door to Ariana's evil world.

"Why don't you ask your little friends, Paige. I'm not helping you with this one."

"Then what are you doing here? I want you to leave, now." I spun around and opened the screen door. "Get out. I don't feel comfortable with you here, and I never gave you permission to come over."

"Oh, it's going to be like that, eh, Paige? You don't control everything, especially not me."

Ariana darted over to me but stopped cold. Her long, straggly, black hair rose up like she'd just received a jolt from a faulty light fixture. I giggled, partly at her ridiculous appearance, but mostly from nerves. I felt another's energy press into the room. The wind picked up inside the kitchen, as if we stood outside in a weak tornado, and it empowered me. Ariana brushed past me and ran from the manor.

"I'll be back when your friends aren't here to help you. Mark my words, I'll be back." She darted down the path in the direction of the guesthouse, her hands flailing at her sides as she went.

Turning to my right, I spied my champion, my protector, Archangel Michael. He gazed at me, his wings in all their glory raised at his sides. What a beautiful sight to behold! "Oh, thank God, literally. You're here. What's she talking about?" I asked.

"Don't be frightened, Paige. You are going to keep me busy. He has instructed me to watch over you since the day at Ariana's house, the day you met Beelzebul. The day she pulled off one of the biggest illusions of all time." Archangel Michael paused thoughtfully, staring at me as I leaned against the kitchen counter, trying to catch my breath. "She mentioned glamouring? I think you're ready now to understand what it is. It's the ability to invoke a spell on someone, an illusion on the eyes of the observer. It's what caused you to believe Brad's mother's house had disappeared. We were merely thrown out the front door, and the house was cloaked with an invisible shield. To the naked eye, it looked like the house had disappeared. Impressive to some, I know. I allowed the spell to happen to gauge Ariana's strength. Her power is growing. I believe you are finally seeing her for who she really is. It's never easy to see the truth about someone and their betrayal. Especially when that someone could have been a new friend. With your gift and sensitivity, I'm afraid you will always have to be careful who you let into your life. God has commissioned two sentinels to stay by your side while you walk through your daily life."

"Wait. Sentinels? I'm almost afraid to ask." I grabbed a glass from the cupboard and poured myself some water.

"Think of them as an early warning system that will set off an alarm and send for us—me, Archangel Raphael, and Gabriel—when you need us most. Faced with evil, it's hard to cry out for help and name us. God has seen to it that the sentinels will. You'll never see them. Think of them as His representatives. You might sense them now and again, but that will be for your peace of mind."

"What do they look like? Can you see them? Please, can you describe them to me?"

"If you must know, they are white dogs. They sit on either side of you, one at each foot. Where you go, they go. Loyal to you and you alone. They will help to guard your safety, Paige. Be happy. God walks with you, with them."

"Oh, my. Sounds pretty surreal to me. Can I pet them?"

"No. They are not that kind of pet. They must be respected and treated like royalty. Just know they're with you and be grateful. Glory be to God."

Poof. Archangel Michael disappeared. I'd always wondered how the spiritual realm worked, and I was beginning to see the protocol of Archangels in response to God's wishes. And now, to have the white dogs guarding me ... well, it was mind-blowing.

CHAPTER SEVENTEEN

Mrs. Jamieson's monotone voice droned on as summer school crawled along at a snail's pace. If I was going to do my best, I'd have to fight my boredom. I'd been granted a second chance and knew I needed to secure my high school diploma. Sadly, I had missed any chance of attending university in September, as all deadlines had passed. I felt out of step with my classmates, and, in some twisted way, I missed Ariana's presence. She haunted me.

Shuddering at this realization, I forced myself to remember the time I saw her with her hair standing on end like she had stuck her finger in a light socket. I wondered what I'd gotten myself into. I should have heeded the warnings from Peggy, Carole, Uncle Kyle, and Grey Owl. After all, they'd been there for me all along. If Dexter could betray me and my family, why couldn't someone like Ariana? I would have to be more careful who I befriended before I took a leap of faith. Being gifted was far more complicated than I had ever imagined.

***

One Saturday, as I lay daydreaming, I heard loud voices and laughter coming from the kitchen. I jumped out of bed, grabbed my favourite pink velour robe with matching slippers, and ran down the hall to find Bradley Allan Parkman standing just inside the door. He looked handsome in his khaki shorts and black T-shirt, sporting a goatee. Brad grinned at me as if he'd just seen his long-lost best friend. His intense, black eyes pierced me to the core.

"Paige, it's so great to see you. I heard about what happened at the old cottage and had to come by and make sure you're okay." Brad stormed over to me and wrapped me tightly in his arms.

I pushed him away, not wanting to betray Allan, my potential new boyfriend.

"Good to see you too, Brad. Why didn't you just call?" With everything that was going on, I'd become highly sensitive, and I was suspicious of people who suddenly popped up in my life. I hadn't heard a word from Brad in ages. *Why now?* I wondered.

"Call you? I'd rather see you. It's been way too long. Plus, I've been trying to reach my mom. She took in some student named Annie ... or Ann or something. I don't remember, but I haven't heard from her in the past two weeks." Tears welled up in Brad's eyes.

"Well, I don't know what's happening. Have you been by the house, yet?" I asked.

"Nope, you're on the way. I was hoping to pick you up so we could go together. That is, if you're not too busy." Brad wiped his tears from his cheeks.

Mixed feelings raged within me — from unthinkable anger, stemming from the day Brad dumped me, to sadness that he didn't know what he was about to get himself into: the world of demons, witchcraft, and fear. How would I ever explain to him about the evil living in his house, threatening the safety of his mom?

Grandpa walked into the room beaming with happiness at the sight of Brad, his buddy. He wrapped Brad in a bear hug and hollered at me over his shoulder, "Why didn't you tell me Brad was here?"

"Sorry, Grandpa. Brad wants me to visit his mom. I'll run and change."

"Of course, Paige." Grandpa turned to Brad and said, "After you have a nice visit with your mom, come back and see us, will you?" He grinned.

"I sure will, Mr. O'Brien."

Brad waited patiently, then smiled when I entered the foyer and opened the door for me. I waved goodbye to my grandparents, wondering if they'd ever see me again after I faced the evil entities squatting at Sarah's house.

We jumped into his truck. I ran my fingers over the familiar vinyl seat.

"This was Dexter's truck, yes?"

"Oh yeah. Your grandparents gave her to me. Isn't Cheyenne great? I love me some classy 1972 Chevy. Remember how Dexter used to say that?" Brad's eyes sparkled at the memory of our beloved friend.

"Nope. Not to me. Glad you have it, Brad." I returned his smile.

"So what's been going on? It's been awhile. I hope things have settled down." Brad's eyes looked hopeful.

"Nothing much." I lied through my teeth, knowing he couldn't handle the truth. I felt it was best to steer him away from anything supernatural on the estate. After all, why would I open the door to the otherworld to Brad if he proclaimed he couldn't handle it?

We rode in silence, and I wondered what sort of explanation I could give to Brad when he met Ariana and saw how evil she was. And I heard, *That girl is poison,* playing on the radio. We turned the corner and headed up the gravel drive. There stood his Victorian-style home, looming against the backdrop of a foreboding, cloudy sky. Sarah's old jalopy, as she called it, was parked in the driveway. I gave my head a shake and worried what demonic scene would unfold next.

"BAPS, you're home!" Sarah said as she barged out the white lattice screen door. "I'm so happy to see you, sweetie. Hi, Paige. C'mon in, you two. So great to see you together." She waved us inside.

Relieved to see Sarah's jovial welcome, I hesitated at the car. "See? There's nothing going on here, Brad. Why don't you go in and visit with your mom? I have somewhere I need to be. Go ahead. I'll walk back."

"Are you sure? I'll come by and see you at the manor before I leave. I've missed you." He reached out for my hand, but I withdrew it before he made contact.

Marching down the drive, I shook my head while talking aloud to myself. "How could this possibly be happening? Glamouring. Humph. One minute the house is there; next minute it's not. And now it's back again. Magic ... " I slapped the top of my head to see if I was trapped in a dream. *Wow, that hurt.*

Before I could take another step, I spied Ariana through the tall, spindly cedar trees and peeked through the branches. She wore a black hooded robe, and I feared she was waiting to kidnap me — or kill me, once and for all. I knelt down for a moment, drawing the sign of the cross on my chest, and collected my thoughts. She marked the ground with a wide circle, using her knife, and drew a six-pointed hexagram, much like a star. Goosebumps raged across my body.

It dawned on me that the battle between good and evil had indeed begun centuries ago. And I was born into this world, at this exact time, living on a semi-isolated estate, to fight for the goodness in the world in the name of humanity. The gravity of the situation hit me. *Why me?* I thought. Surely there were plenty of others more qualified to carry out this monumental undertaking.

CHAPTER EIGHTEEN

Conall and Mackenzie watched in despair as Paige floundered, a brave soul trying to resolve the biggest challenge of all time. They were saddened that their opportunity to help their friend had passed. Throughout Paige's time of need, they were commanded not to interfere with her destiny, yet Mackenzie had defied the orders. She had taken a huge risk when she informed Paige that Ariana did indeed practice black magic. And now Mackenzie was suffering the consequences. No further communication was sanctioned. This troubled Mackenzie. It was worse than death itself, to watch as a beloved human being suffered her fate. Paige seemed frozen in time as she hid in the bushes.

"If we aren't sanctioned to assist Paige, what else can we do to help her?" asked Mackenzie. She strolled along wearing her white jumper with fabric eyelets adorning her waistline, a baby-blue ribbon tying back her blonde hair. So serious for a young earthbound.

"Unless we're told we can help, we have to hang back, Mackenzie. I know; I'm also at a loss. I thought we were here to help, not to sit back and watch as Paige is tormented and physically abused. I don't understand it at all."

Conall reached out and held his sister's hand. It was the first time Mackenzie felt comforted in a long time. "All we can do now, sister, is pray for Paige and her family and hope that God, Gabriel, and the Archangels Michael and Raphael come to her aid when she needs it most. Don't forget she has her two sentinels guarding her now. That's all we can do, Mackenzie. We must let this go as ordered."

"So be it then," *Mackenzie said.*

Brother and sister walked hand in hand into the light. Their mother, Sasha Grace, waited to greet them.

"Come, my children, I will guide you home to Heaven. There is no sin in wanting to help those we love. But you were instructed not to do so. Now, I will stand by your side. Our Heavenly Father will forgive you. He is a loving God. It is sanctioned," *said Sasha Grace.*

CHAPTER NINETEEN

While texting Carole, I experienced a nudging, like someone pushing me on the arm, urging me towards my photo lab in the basement of O'Brien Manor. I had so many memories of that place, and they weren't the good kind. I wondered why I would be summoned there, to the isolated place in the basement. Images floated through my mind, images that made me want to flee from the manor: a vague memory of Conall tossing Brad against the wall outside my darkroom; the vision experienced in the ice vault room of the young boy being tortured by his father; the hellhounds congregating at the bottom of the stairs. I awaited a response from Carole, but guessed she was too busy to reply.

As if someone was pulling me by my hand, I made my way to the three-quarter length door, pulled out the skeleton key gifted from Grandma, and unlocked the door with a loud click. I tugged on the overhead chain and heard a clink as the lights sparked to life, thankful they worked this time. As I descended the stairs, my footsteps echoed around me. I stopped to listen and found the silence reassuring. I was alone ... or so I hoped.

I reached the stone-cold cement floor and headed for my darkroom. I smiled as I was reminded of my grandparents' kindness once again; they had the lab renovated for me, after all. The familiar musty scent shot a pang to my heart. I cranked on the doorknob and flicked on the lights. There was my favourite rectangular table, handcrafted by Dexter from an antique barn door. Nothing had changed since I last left the room. Feeling at home, I checked my photography equipment and *snap!* I realized a distraction from my everyday problems was just what I needed. I loved developing photos. It was engrossing work and would leave no time for wondering about all the spooky things happening on the estate.

As I touched the developer, a vision slammed into my mind, memories of the day a nasty earthbound banged on the locked door trying to bust it down. My prayers for help had been answered right away. I'd watched a whirlwind appear out of nowhere and rip through the room. As the door burst open, the winds swept the black shadow away. Now, looking back, I realized what I thought was an earthbound was, in fact, a demon. Perhaps I was guided to my photo studio to connect the dots regarding what was really haunting the O'Brien estate.

Ping! A short text from Carole noted that Uncle Kyle was helping her dad plant some herbs necessary for his wellness store.

I texted a reply. *No worries. It can wait.*

He's asking how he can help, Carole texted a minute later.

Realizing a face-to-face was necessary, I asked Carole to let me know when the three of us could get together. She promised to get back to me as soon as she could.

It was time for me to gather my thoughts and figure out exactly what I needed from Uncle Kyle, the elder. I couldn't fathom the knowledge he must have. I decided to ask him about the dream I had of my baptism at the brook and the connection I felt with the grandfather rock. *What is it?* I knew it had healed me ... but how, exactly?

Suddenly, I sensed strong spirit energy in the room and saw a vague image of a man wearing a fringed jacket and matching fringed pants. I sensed sorrow in his piercing brown eyes. He had a long, thin, pointed nose, and his lips were pressed into a fine line, accentuating his cheekbones. Long, tidy hair draped loosely over his shoulders. I noticed a beaver at his feet. It had the most beautiful, bushy coat of glossy brown fur and a wide, flat tail. Then the man spoke to me, his voice gentle and kind.

Paige, I am Grey Owl. The Grey Owl you know is my name-sake. The grandfather rocks are as old as time on earth. They must be respected, for they hold the key to all that has happened in this world from generation to generation, a link to the ancient world. Kyle explained to you once that you must tend to your garden, as it is a human's relationship with the earth that is most important. Tend to it, nurture it, and you will reap what it sows. Grandfather rocks are individual rocks that have memories dating back to before humankind existed. Some believe the secrets of Earth's healing powers lie therein. Next time you place your hand on the the grandfather rock, the healing rock, it may awaken some visions within you. They're a conduit to our Creator. They'll help you to understand what you must do in order to survive the demons' threat. Our ancestors want to help you, too.

When his spirit vanished, I slumped down onto an antique wooden bench and pondered what Grey Owl had revealed to me. I reflected on my visits to the brook. Sometimes while seated on a rock, I experienced peacefulness followed by an energetic burst, like I'd been rejuvenated. Of course, I attributed this to sitting near the calming water. Could it be that the O'Brien estate was built upon many of these ancient grandfather rocks, and was once considered sacred First Nations' land? Perhaps, now the rocks act as a conduit between the otherworld and the human world, our world? One word popped into my mind as if typed on a ticker tape:

BINGO! Before I could think more about it, light footsteps in the hall aroused my attention and my right ear half-cocked. I was interrupted by a knock on my lab door.

"I understand you need to speak to me," Uncle Kyle said. "It sounded urgent. Your grandfather let me in. I hope you don't mind. Carole urged me to come. She's worried about you." His stocky build filled the entryway and if I didn't know him well enough, I might have been intimidated. Instead, I jumped up to greet him.

"Thank you so much for coming!" I said.

"What's wrong, Paige? You look like you've seen a ghost."

"I may have. I'm confused. I was visited by Grey Owl's spirit. The one your friend is named after. How can that be? And then you appeared." I stared intently at him awaiting his response. "Our Grey Owl isn't ... he's not dead, is he? Why didn't he come and explain to me about the grandfather rocks?"

Uncle Kyle smiled and said, "Oh no, Paige. Remember he told us he was going to the brook to ask for our ancestors' help? Perhaps he asked the spirit he was named after, and often seeks guidance from, to visit you. The original Grey Owl. Though our ancestor wasn't a blood First Nation, he lived as one, married an Ojibwe woman, and had great wisdom. He was adopted as one of the Native peoples and inherited the name *Washaquonasin,* meaning great grey owl in Ojibwe. Until the day he died, he was accepted as a blood native." Uncle Kyle paused for a second. "What did he say when he spoke to you?"

"Grey Owl explained about grandfather rocks and how ancient they are. Perhaps they hold the key to ancient wisdom."

"Many say they do, Paige. Have you been granted wisdom from the grandfather rock near the brook?" asked Uncle Kyle. "Please, let me help you."

"Each time I've gone for a healing in the past, I've felt energized and healed. But the last time I was there, the wise man with white hair tied in two braids guided me to ask your friend, Grey Owl, and you about the grandfather rocks. Then the spirit of the original Grey Owl appeared just before you arrived and explained them to me. The wise man predicted that the next time I touch the grandfather rock, I will receive messages about how to use its wisdom to help battle the evil on the estate. I'm not sure what's going to happen, but I better be ready for it. Funny ... I had a vision, and it revealed that you are vital in guiding me and helping me decipher signs that will help in the final battle over evil. And here you are."

"I will help you in any way I can," promised Uncle Kyle. "You definitely are the Chosen One, Paige, chosen to resolve this conflict between our world and the underworld." He looked directly into my eyes. "I know evil is creeping into your life, into our world, and we must stop it dead in its tracks, pardon the pun." He smiled and tried to lighten the mood.

"I know, and I'm trying to figure this out for myself, but I need everyone's help, including the Archangels and— "

"Our Creator, Paige. Nothing can be done without His approval. It is He you are fighting for, after all. You are the chosen warrior. I will help you in any way I can, as will my family and our ancestors. This Ariana who has come into your life, who is she?"

I was shocked to hear that Uncle Kyle knew of her. "I met her in the hospital when I was recuperating. She lives with Sarah Parkman, Brad's mom. Do you know the family?"

"I've heard of them. Please, go on."

"And she practices black magic."

"Aww... there's the piece of the puzzle I wasn't expecting. Paige, magic is magic. It's what's in the practitioner's heart that guides whether the magic is perceived or intended as good or bad. But it's something to be wary of. Magic has been performed since the beginning of time. It is documented back to biblical times; even Moses was rumoured to be a magician of sorts. But it should only be practiced if gifted by our Creator to those pure of heart. He bestows this honour upon the chosen. And let's be clear—it's to be used for goodness, not evil. But many believe magic is for anyone to practice for their own personal goals and needs or desires. This is just not the case. Those chosen to perform magic must be trained by their elders. It is a gruelling process. Many who pursue magic are not the chosen ones. That's where the trouble begins. How is she doing this ... magic?"

"She has a creepy diary. It's huge, with bones along the edges."

Uncle Kyle leaned back against the door. "You mean she has access to a grimoire, a spellbook that she hasn't been granted formal access to?"

"Yes. Now I know why I often feel sick to my stomach. In my gut, I know evil has been unleashed upon our estate, heightened by Ariana's presence and her use of the grimoire." I rubbed the side of my neck in order to calm myself.

"She must be stopped! At all costs. How can I help, Paige?"

"How do we get the grimoire away from her? She spoke about King Solomon and some book he wrote, called a Testament. And she's obsessed with some ring with the Seal of Solomon. I searched the internet for it. Apparently, Solomon's father, King David, had a seal made using his initials and a hexagram, and this seal was passed along to his son. Solomon redesigned the seal with a three-dimensional hexagram, a six-pointed star with interwoven triangles. He used the seal inscribed with the Tetragrammaton. It took me a lot of digging to discover what the Tetragrammaton is. It's the biblical Hebrew name for God, which are the initials YHWH—*Yod, He, Waw, He*—meaning *to exist* or *will be*. To pronounce it, it sounds like Yahweh. You probably know a lot about this... those four letters were mentioned in the 2000-year-old Dead Sea Scrolls."

"Yes, I've come across this information in my travels. But, please continue."

"Anyways, Solomon sealed the demons in brass vessels using lead caps. He would stamp the lids with the seal on his ring and imprison the jinn, or spirits, and cast them into the ocean. To me, it sounds like the legendary genie in the bottle from the Aladdin stories. Were those genies actually demons ... ? No matter. Solomon was granted these magical powers from God through Archangel Michael to ward off demons and grant protection against their evil influence and control them. Unfortunately, it didn't seem to work very well, because King Solomon became a sinner. Wait, I get it now. You're so right! It's in the bearer's heart which way the magic is used—for good or for evil. I don't think it's the actual magic that is dark or black; it's what's in the person's heart." I grabbed two bottles of water from the mini-fridge and handed one to him. "Archangel Michael explained it to me." I threw my arms up into the air, exasperated. "I feel like I'm smack dab in the middle of a fairy tale."

"That's a lot to process. Things just keep getting more and more interesting by the day, don't they? No wonder Carole is praying constantly for you and for help from our Creator. At first I thought she was a bit jealous of your new friend, Ariana. Now I know she saw through her from the beginning. That niece of mine is definitely gifted." Uncle Kyle flicked his long, black braid and touched the white eagle feather in his hair. "Well, my friend, I think you must go to the brook and have a communion with our ancestors using the grandfather rock. That would be my next step, if I stood in your shoes."

"Good call. I will. I'm long overdue for a healing and must continue with my protection prayers, too. For everyone's sake." As he motioned for me to exit the room ahead of him, I placed my hand on his arm and said, "Thank you for being so compassionate."

"No thanks needed. We're all connected. I'm here when you need me."

"Well, I am honoured to have your help in this matter, along with both Grey Owls."

I could not stop myself as I counted 167 steps to the kitchen, realizing my obsessive-compulsive disorder I thought I had overcome, had indeed returned. My anxiety was at an all time high and my compulsions took over. I began to count my steps again. We reached the kitchen only to find it was empty. Uncle Kyle put his hand on the kitchen door knob and hesitated.

"I think I have an idea, Paige. I can't tell you just yet, but I will ask my brother." And on that note, he rushed out the door.

I heard soft footsteps in the hallway followed by Grandma's engaging entrance as she flung her right hand up and pointed her finger around the room. "Paige, where's your company?" she asked, searching the kitchen. "I heard Carole's uncle's baritone voice."

"He just left. Sorry, Grandma. I hate to keep running out on you but I've something to do. I'll be back later."

I hurried to my bedroom and changed into my navy blue running shorts and a lime green tee with the words *Stand up for Yourself* printed across the front. I loved statement T-shirts. I slipped on my favourite running shoes in anticipation of some exercise and left the manor through the east entrance. I jogged for awhile to clear my head, slowing only when the rays from the hot July sun sapped my energy. As I arrived at Peggy's cottage , I sensed she wasn't home and had a brief vision of her out shopping, her purse in hand. Clamouring up her steps, I rapped hard and waited. Just as

I thought, there was no reply. I was delighted when I heard the crunch of tires on the driveway and turned around to find a dark brown SUV approaching, Carole at the wheel. She pulled to an abrupt stop, and Peggy climbed from the passenger seat with bags of groceries in each arm.

"Carole, Peggy!" I exclaimed but I was too late. Carole roared out of the driveway in a cloud of dust. It was the first time I had seen her ride, a dark brown SUV ... especially useful in our extreme Canadian winters.

Peggy dropped a bag of groceries. "Good golly. Paige, dear, will you help me bring these inside? Carole needed to get home."

"Of course." I ran over to help Peggy. "Where's she going in such a hurry?"

"I'm not really sure. Something about her uncle asking her dad for help. Thanks, Paige. Give me a minute to get up the porch steps."

Peggy shuffled by me, holding onto the railing for support.

"Happy to help. You go in ahead," I offered, politely, while juggling the bags of groceries.

Peggy shook her head, held the screen door, and motioned me inside. I thought it odd that she wouldn't lock her door.

Humans aren't the problem around here, Paige.

I laughed aloud at Peggy's message. As I brushed past her, I felt a pang of guilt for not being in touch more. I said over my shoulder, "Can we have a chat in your communications room after I put these groceries away?"

"Of course, dear. I'll open it up and fluff the cushions. Come in when you're done. And thank you again for your help."

Groceries put away in their respective cupboards and refrigerator — check. Tea brewed, steeped, and poured — check. I loaded up the tray and was happy with myself for finding Peggy's famous coconut squares too.

"I took the liberty of grabbing us some squares with our tea, Peggy. I hope you don't mind. It's so great to be here. I've been bombarded with homework. Thanks for the break in my day."

"Happy to have a visit with you. I was hoping you'd find them ... the squares. I make them just for you and Carole. Now let's get down to business. What's troubling you, Paige?"

"Ha ha. You get right to it."

"Things have grown serious upon the estate. And I'm never really sure how long we'll have together."

"Well, it seems you're right about Ariana. She's more troubled than I had perceived. I thought she was just a misunderstood, adopted, only child, but I was wrong. She practices magic ... the dark kind." There. I said it aloud. And I knew once it was out there, there was no turning back with Peggy.

"This is worse than I thought. What is she using to practice spells from, if I may ask?"

"Like I told Uncle Kyle, it's a grimoire. He says it's a powerful book of magic."

"I know of them. If she's using a grimoire and is searching for the original Testament, we're all in big trouble," Peggy said. "It can do more harm than anyone could ever imagine. That's the darkness I feel now. We have to stop her, Paige, and fast."

"I understand, but how exactly?" Then I received a telepathic message from Carole.

You must come to my home and meet with my dad. He can help us. As soon as you're done at Peggy's.

I straightened up on the floral love seat and noticed Peggy had moved her feet from the ottoman and was now perched upon the edge of her rocking chair.

"Well, I can see you received a message of sorts. What is it?" she asked. Her blue eyes appeared soulful and filled with love, and her wrinkled face reflected all the wisdom of her years. She was a lovely woman, inside and out, due in large part, I assumed, to the fact that she lived a healthy life free of the vices most humans battled.

Snapping back to the question at hand, I answered, "Carole invited me over to meet her dad. He has some news, I guess. I've never met him before. Have you?"

"Yes, of course. He's a wise elder and shaman in the Aamjiwnaang band. If he's offering his help, we are lucky indeed. Few non-native people are invited to his estate. It is rumoured to be an ancient sacred meeting place of many First Nations people. Because of the medicine bundle they created for you, I assume they're inviting you as a fellow native. This is great news, Paige. Go now, you need all the help you can get."

"I didn't know you knew about the medicine bundle." As I spoke, I also became aware of the fact that I didn't know the way to Carole's house, and I would be travelling alone.

On that thought, Peggy added, "You'll know, Paige. Just follow the path leading out my side door to the south of here, through the forest. You'll see, and probably more importantly, you'll know you're on the right path." Peggy smiled at me. "Oh, I may have telepathically figured it out about the bundle. You don't mind, do you?"

"No. I don't know what I'd do without you." I slurped the last sip of my tea and got to my feet, ready to be on my way.

"Wait!" Peggy said as I headed for the door. "There's one more thing. I'll be right back."

I watched in amusement as she scurried from the room. Her bright floral dress reminded me of Hanna's style and it made me feel safe for some reason. I guessed it was the grandmother factor. I listened as her footsteps echoed down the hallway. In the meantime, I picked a book from her bookshelf called *Travels* by the movie producer and writer of *Jurassic Park*, Michael Crichton, and randomly flipped through it, landing on a page with the words *astral travel*. The subject grabbed my attention. Just as I began to read, I heard Peggy's footsteps in the hall again. I earmarked the page in the hopes of returning to read more about the intriguing subject later.

"I almost forgot. You must take some tobacco with you. Don't worry, Carole will explain," Peggy said, a bit out of breath.

"Are you okay?" I asked, concerned her years were catching up with her after all.

"I'm fine. It's the humidity. It gets to me at this time of year but it passes next month, late August." Peggy offered up a big smile, probably trying to allay my fears.

I sniffed the pouch; the scent was powerful and zoomed straight up my nostrils. Scrunching up my nose, I said, "Thank you, Peggy. This is going to be quite an adventure."

Smiling as I stared into her twinkling blue eyes, I listened as her cheerful laughter steadied my nerves. She patted my arm and sent me on my way. Peggy was indeed one of my most loyal, trusted friends and mentors.

CHAPTER TWENTY

While jogging to Carole's house, I felt the stress slip away. There was no other natural high like it in the world to me; it was invigorating. I sensed animated spirits accompanying me on my journey, an excited energy much like children running and laughing alongside me. Butterflies fluttered in my stomach as I anticipated meeting Carole's dad, at long last, but I revelled in the fact that help from my loyal friends awaited.

My attention turned to the well-manicured trail. It was about four feet wide, preserved with fragrant wood chips, and had a healthy forest on either side. I hadn't seen this sort of path since I was a child when I hiked with my parents at the Cyprus Lake Grotto, about one hundred and eighty-six miles north of Camlachie. The Grotto is a massive cave carved along the shores of Georgian Bay; it took more than a thousand years to form. My favourite memory was of the day Mom and I climbed down and into the cave. We tackled the outside wall that jutted over Georgian Bay and, from there, climbed inside the cave. It was tricky but well worth seeing the turquoise water and the beauty of the natural grotto. The trail leading to the Grotto was constructed by local volunteers, and they filled the path with wood chips to soak up the excess rain water.

Feeling less stressed with my happy childhood memory, my thoughts strayed. I wondered why I had never met Carole's dad before. And then I remembered her mom had died over a year ago. Perhaps that was the answer. People grieve in their own way, and I was not one to judge. It took me a long time to get over Dexter's death, and I knew in my heart I would always carry his love and good memories with me. He was my protector ... until the darkness set into him. Even the most faithful can fall prey to the tomfoolery of demons or earthbounds, if not careful — especially in our vulnerable times.

As the trail twisted and turned, I fell in love with the nature surrounding me. Pine and oak trees, maples, and tall cedars unfolded before me. I came upon an emerald lake with four canoes parked on its shores. Beside them was a fire pit surrounded by sizable rocks. I pictured people sitting on them. In the distance I spied two rows of wooden benches, eight in total, separated by an aisle. I wondered who would create such an intimate setting and what it might be used for.

As much as I enjoyed the scenery, I thought I should've arrived at Carole's by now. Grabbing my cell phone from my pocket, I noticed it had been fifteen minutes since I left Peggy's house. *Why didn't I ask her how long this would take?* A narrow wooden footbridge crossed a creek ahead. I ran to it just in time to watch two beautiful white trumpeter swans float by, headed for the lake with four babies, cygnets, in tow. It warmed my heart. I leaned over the bridge's wooden railing and soaked in every detail. I breathed deeply, taking in as much as I could of the forest's dewy scent, enjoying the serenity of the moment.

After my soul-filling, nature-viewing moment, I approached what appeared to be a dead end on the path — a wall of cedar trees. Panic set in and I skipped a breath until I saw the path veered to the left. And there it was in all its glory, a log cabin and fields of planted herbs.

As I approached the house, I heard Carole cry, "Stop. I'll be right there." She ran to me, almost tripping as she slipped on her sandals amidst running.

"What's the problem?" I yelled back to her. No answer. *Patience, Paige.*

"Hi, Paige. Sorry for the cloak-and-dagger. Humour me, okay?" Carole's voice cracked.

"Okay, what's up?" I scanned the grounds, wondering if a big dog or something worse was going to leap out at me, and a bit of sweat broke out on my brow. *Have a little faith, Paige.*

"When you visit our home," she began, panting as she spoke, "you must say a prayer, like the day my uncle suggested to you to say prayers that relate to you and your family before you open your medicine bundle. Well, we say an Ojibwe prayer to our Creator and our land. It's really only necessary on your first visit, okay? Unless you choose to do it again. Never mind." Carole shook her head. "But it's very important. We chant. Repeat after me:

> *Who dares without tobacco?*
> *Who dares without offering?*
> *Fill my spirit with goodness, so my life may be upright.*
> *Defend my heart against evil so that I may prevail."*

I stared at Carole for a moment before speaking. I knew this was a very special moment.

"C'mon, Paige. It's okay. Repeat it back with me, okay? Let's say it together and repeat it twice." And we did exactly that. "Okay, now lay the pouch of tobacco on the ground." Carole struck a match, and lit the tobacco on fire. "This is done in honour of our land, our peoples, Creator, and for the blessing and protection of our souls. There now. It's almost out. Time for you to meet my dad." Carole dug a small trench around the tobacco to prevent a brush fire.

"This is the first time I've been a witness and participant in your culture. It's beautiful, Carole. Thank you for letting me be a part of it." I welled up for a moment but wiped away the tears. "With all that's been going on lately, thank you for this. I mean ... I really needed it, and now I feel lighter after chanting with you. And I loved running along the path. Fantabulous! It's so tranquil and undisturbed."

Carole gave me a reassuring nod and said, "Follow me. As the song says, you ain't seen nothing yet." She led the way around the planted fields and skirted some rather large rocks.

"Carole, are those grandfather rocks?" I asked.

She just smiled. "Hurry!"

Carole asked me to remove my shoes before entering their family's home, the largest log cabin I had ever seen. We marched through a mud room, into an exotic room centred around a spectacular tree. There was an overpowering energy that left me a bit overwhelmed. Brown suede couches encircled the tree, with enough seating for fifteen to twenty people.

The inside of the home was much more spacious than I'd expected, but I wasn't surprised to see plants and flowers everywhere, providing the perfect feng shui. But even more curious than all of this, there was no TV. *Hmmm ... Like Peggy's communications room*, I thought. Carole smiled at me. *What is this room, Carole?* I asked.

Please wait for my father, she replied.

A man emerged from a hallway on the other side of the log cabin. He had long, beautiful black hair and had a multicoloured bandana wrapped around his forehead. His black dress shirt and pants revealed his toned physique, and he wore caramel-coloured moccasins. His intense, dark, brown eyes, wide nose, large mouth, and tanned face were striking.

"There you are, Carole. And you've finally brought Paige around to meet your old dad. So happy to have you in our home. Welcome!" He walked towards me with perfect posture, held out his hand to shake mine, and as we grasped each other, an electrical shock shot straight up my arm. I gasped. "It's okay, Paige. Please don't be alarmed. You might call that electrostatic energy. We shared an electrical charge between two very spiritual friends." He gave me a reassuring nod. "Please call me Wayne."

"No worries," I blurted out. "Nice to finally meet you, sir … Wayne. You're really busy with your alternative healthcare, I mean, wellness business. Carole has mentioned it." I graciously bowed my head, not understanding what moved me to do so.

"I'm never too busy for family and friends. Our wellness business is near and dear to our hearts. You know about the Aamjiwnaang First Nations lands and how sick they are. That's why I moved my family to Camlachie. But …" Wayne paused, a wistful look in his eyes. "Anyways, it was too late for Carole's mother, my wife, Lily, but now I can help others. I feel if someone is ill and they are given the right herb in the right dosage, it is the key to better health. Mind, body, and soul. Anyways, Paige, I have an odd request. May I smudge you? You know, run a sage stick up and down your aura."

"Of course. I've heard about it but never had it done before." I watched as Carole's dad lit a sage stick and blew on the end of it, extinguishing the flame and allowing the smoke to billow.

"Carole, go get my clay bowl, please. It's fireproof … very important," he said. "This will just take a few minutes," he instructed, as he ran the sage slowly up and down and around my body. "Now raise your arms, please."

I obeyed but noticed the smoke had thickened. "Is this normal?" I asked. "The amount of smoke, I mean."

"Well, let's just say there's some negativity around you. But that should come as no surprise, right? With all that's been going on at the estate."

"I guess so," I answered, feeling uneasy. Somehow seeing the smoke billow around me put me on edge.

"Okay, you're all clear. Come and have a seat." Wayne walked over to Carole and laid the sage stick in the bowl and then carried it over to a writing desk, making sure he set it down carefully. "Never extinguish a sage wand if you ever do this, Paige. It must finish its course of action. At least that's how we do it. But be careful not to leave it unattended. It will eventually burn out." Next, he patted one of the couches and said, "You can sit here. You've said your prayers?" He peered into my eyes, awaiting my response.

"Oh, yes ... of course," I murmured. His energy was intense.

Carole nudged me forward, and we sat together facing the magnificent tree. "It's beautiful isn't it? Dad had our home built around the old oak tree. Get it?" she asked, elbowing me. "My mom used to sing that archaic song *Tie a Yellow Ribbon*. Have you heard it?"

I shook my head.

"Tie a yellow ribbon round the ole oak tree," Carole sang, laughing. I saw tears in her eyes, and she quickly looked away. "Anyways, it's unique ... the tree, I mean, and probably more than a hundred and fifty years old, judging by the size of its trunk. My dad had a special sloped roof designed to allow for part of the tree to grow above our roofline and a rubber collar system installed. It's a big hole with a rubber rain catcher that takes the rain overflow into a downspout. It stops the rain from dripping into our house. Cool, eh? My mom loved it so. The tree I mean." Carole stopped talking and stared at her dad.

"I remember, Carole," her dad added softly, walking over to give his daughter a comforting pat. "But let's help Paige today. Did you explain to her about the prayers, why we recite them before walking on the land or entering our home?"

"Not really. I thought you should explain all of it." Carole gave a nervous giggle.

"Of course," Wayne said. "I'd be pleased to." Then he focused his attention on me. "Paige, this is a sacred place from centuries ago, a dedicated land for all our people to come together to practice healing rituals, perform dance ceremonies, share ideas and information. What you may know as grandfather rocks are found throughout our fifteen acres of property. It's well-known amongst the First Nations people far and wide. It's a healing place of sorts. Do you feel anything different while here, Paige?"

I glanced around the room and spied a white eagle feather in a pebbled glass vase. I heard, *Eagle feathers connect us to the spirituality of the eagle. He connects us to our Creator and provides visions for us. Upon touching the eagle feather, cleansing and healing can begin.* I smiled at Carole, thankful for her telepathic explanation. "I just feel like I don't want to leave, I guess. It's so warm and peaceful. I feel like I'm surrounded by a cloud of love." I shrugged.

"Wonderful!" Wayne said. "We say prayers to honour our Creator and our ancestry. I understand you're ready to meet one of our grandfather rocks. Come."

We followed Wayne from the cabin, and he led us to a clearing with a ginormous rock similar to the brook's red, yellow, black, and white grandfather rock. I reached out to touch it; Carole grabbed my arm.

"Sorry. My dad has to explain something to you first," Carole whispered.

"I've been called upon to introduce you, Paige, to this grandfather rock. Many come from all over to listen to its messages and to receive its healings. It has the wisdom of the ancients. Before you ever touch it, you must kneel next to it and say your prayers, like my brother Kyle has instructed you to do. Then steady yourself with your breathing; breathe in, hold for four, and breathe out, hold for four. Do it a few times. Once you feel steady, grounded, you may reach out and place your left hand — your receiving hand that allows a spiritual connection — on the rock, being careful not to lose your balance. Sometimes the energy is ... well, it's overpowering and can knock you over if you're not careful." With that, Wayne stepped away. "This is where we depart. You will receive your blessings, healings, or messages undisturbed. Come on, Carole. Paige'll be just fine."

Carole and her dad strolled away arm in arm. I was happy to see my BFF had such a close relationship with her dad. I turned towards the grandfather rock and wondered what would happen to me when I connected with it. I felt a bit apprehensive, as it was much bigger than any I had ever seen. I was trained by Grey Owl and Uncle Kyle on the protocol, so I figured that part should be a cinch.

After I recited the Lord's Prayer and Psalm 23, I did the breathing technique. Then, as instructed, I placed my left hand on the grandfather rock. I immediately heard the words, *Welcome, my child. You've come at last. You are in spiritual warfare and we are here to help you. Your healing begins now.* A tingling moved up my arm and travelled my body from head to toe. Completely relaxed, I fell backwards onto my butt. Sudden wooziness crept in and I felt light-headed. I lay down on the ground and stared up at the cloudy sky until I crashed.

A blinding sun sat high in the sky overhead, and the cry of an eagle awakened my senses. Perched on the edge of a cliff, my wings outstretched, I plunged forward into the air, a resounding screech echoed throughout the valley. It was a magnificent moment, and I truly felt my spirit had been set free.

Snapping out of the vision, I bolted upright and brushed myself off. My only thought was, *What will Carole and her dad think about me as an eagle in my vision*?

On my walk back to the cabin, I enjoyed the view of patches of yellow flowers with a black eye in the middle, aptly named black-eyed Susan. It was mom's favourite flower. There were scads of sunflowers blowing in the breeze, and I spied a field of lavender, my favourite herb for curbing my anxiety. The smell alone was a calming influence. Note to self: *Ask Carole if I can take some home.* Boy would I need it now with events on the estate brewing.

My mind drifted back to the day Uncle Kyle taught me how to tend our garden and use some of its flowers for fortifying our health. Crushed up sunflowers were applied to blisters for healing. Good to know when I wandered the grounds of O'Brien Manor. Turning to my right, I swiftly arrived at the cabin and rapped lightly on the door awaiting a response. A few minutes later, I knocked again. Wayne greeted me with a smile.

He looked at his watch and said, "Well, you must have lots to share. If you want to, that is. Come in, please." He pointed to the shoe stand, and I quickly removed mine. I sensed Wayne's peaceful energy as he led the way to the tree room where Carole was waiting.

"Paige, what took you so long?" she asked wide-eyed, her brow furrowed.

I checked my cell phone; it had been three hours since I left. I gasped. "No, it can't be. I'm so sorry. I didn't realize I was gone that long."

"Have a seat, Paige. Quick now, Carole, grab our friend a glass of water. How did it go?" Wayne asked as he perched on the end of the couch and patted my arm.

"No! Wait for me," Carole hollered from the hallway.

"We best wait," Wayne said with a chuckle. He began to pace the floor.

Carole was back in a flash with a mug of cold water. I laughed out loud when I saw the hand-painted image on the side: a bald eagle in flight. "You must know what I'm about to tell you, Carole."

"Not really. Please, go on." She winked at her dad as she added, "Oh, and you can have some of the lavender to take home."

"Ha ha. Thank you so much. Well, I had a vision of a bald eagle flying off the edge of a cliff and releasing its piercing cry. But the eagle was me. And I've had this vision before, and also, another dream ... I saw a man talking to you, Carole. All of a sudden an eagle appeared overhead and dropped a brown feather. The man picked it up and tucked it into your hair."

"Most interesting," Wayne said. "Eagle spirituality is very powerful. Many feel the eagle is a messenger from our Creator. He's sending messages to you in many different ways. You are a true warrior in our midst. The eagle awakens our psychic abilities and enables us to hear spiritual messages. Clarity is part of the gift bestowed upon you, as you perceive things with a more global understanding rather than in a more singular experience. As you soar with your eagle, you must stay grounded and cleanse yourself by the brook. Eagle spirituality also teaches us to respect the freedom of others; the freedom of ourselves, to choose our own paths; it teaches patience ... a word I imagine you're hearing a lot. Our Creator helps us to evolve to a higher place free of the love for our belongings. And through the eagle, teaches us to be mindful when we speak to others, gives us an awareness of how our words can cut others like a knife; the eagle teaches us to be our best selves without inflicting harm on another person. I believe your spirit wolf has taught you all the lessons you needed—balance between self, family, and community. Now you soar with the eagle."

As I listened to Wayne's thoughtful explanation, I heard, *Listen to Elder Wayne George. He is another spirit guide for you to call upon in this turbulent time.*

"It's no coincidence that the O'Brien estate is plagued with earthbounds, demons, and more," said Wayne. "Have you noticed any other spiritual activity on the estate?"

"Well ... there have been hellhounds."

Wayne clapped his hands and interjected, "That makes sense! Hellhounds are charged with protecting cemeteries of families like yours. Something has upset the balance on the estate; that would be the only reason they would join your ranks and help you in this battle to restore balance. It happens every century; evil sneaks into our lands from the underworld."

"Oh my!" I began to pace. "It makes sense somehow. I wondered why the hellhounds would ever rise up with me. They're trying to keep the demons trapped in the underworld and protect my ancestors." Wanting to change the subject, I added, "I thought our souls ... well ... leave our body when we die and are carried up to Heaven with the help of angels or our ancestors. Beyond that, I haven't given it much thought. What does happen to us after we die?" Suddenly, I felt very self-conscious.

"Please, Paige! No more," Carole pleaded. "Death is a morbid topic. It makes me sick just thinking about it."

"Well, aren't I a goof? Sorry, Carole." I looked down, ashamed of myself for speaking about the afterlife when she had lost her mother, one of the most important people in her life, and in her dad's life too.

Wayne spoke passionately as he turned to his daughter. "Death is as natural as birth, *nindaanis*, my daughter. It should be discussed among families. We must prepare ourselves for this eventuality. And it's easier on our family and relatives if we discuss funeral arrangements, rituals, and the afterlife. I don't see death as an end, but as a continuation of our soul's journey. Many believe it's a time to celebrate the release of the soul to return home again."

Surprising myself, I added, "I think most people believe when we die, we die. That's it. Nothing. Darkness. But I've seen and spoken to deceased friends like Dexter. I've heard about and been the victim of earthbound hauntings like … from Bradford. I've been guided by Archangel Michael. I believe there is more to this world than what we see in front of our noses. But not everyone experiences this. Why is that?" I waited eagerly for his response.

"That's a tough question, Paige. And I can only speak from my experiences. Not everyone is in the same phase of their spiritual enlightenment. There are those who open up to the universe's signs. Take numbers, for instance. Some see recurring numbers on a clock, like 1:11 or 3:33 and wonder what their meaning is. They begin to see it everywhere. On license plates or a phone number. It's definitely our Creator waking them up to their psychic abilities. Some say it's the angels, but I believe it's our Creator sanctioning their gift, and He asks the angels to help communicate with those in spiritual self-discovery. The numbers are for reflection, meaning the human seeing them must stop and remember what they were just thinking about when they see these recurring numbers. And each recurring number has individual meaning. If one is open to these signs, their abilities grow, evolve, expand. Sometimes, they begin to sense or see earthbounds, or ghosts, as many like to refer to them. There is definitely a spiritual realm on Earth that is in need of help, and they are reaching out to any and all who can perceive them. It's not always a bad or malignant spirit. Often they are earthbounds lost or trapped in this dimension. And that's what I call hell. But then, there are many people who are skeptical, who hide behind science. People are waking up once again to the understanding that science and spirituality can co-exist and help us to understand the order of our universe. Well, I think that's enough for today. I'm sure you're missed at home, Paige. Your parents will wonder what you're doing."

"Thank you so much for helping me," I said nodding at both Wayne and Carole. "I feel much better now. I'm grateful I can talk to you about these things. You really helped me, Wayne. And I'm sure you're right. My parents will be angry if I don't make it home for supper."

Carole and her dad bid me goodbye, and I hurried out the door and along the wood chip trail, breaking into a run when I reached the gravel road to home. Along the way, my thoughts turned to the conversation I'd had with Wayne. I had gained a more vivid understanding of my spiritual nature and was forever grateful for my First Nations friends. Wayne's insights were priceless, as were Uncle Kyle's and those of both Grey Owls. I was becoming more at peace with myself and my gifts: clairvoyance—seeing visions through my mind's eye; clairsentience—feeling other people's emotions (some call us empaths or intuitives); clairaudience— hearing a quiet whisper in my head telling me what I need to know; and claircognizance—a knowing about something with no logical explanation of how ... all rolled into one package. Though we all have the ability to harness our sixth sense, I felt my most powerful weapon was the ability to talk to spirits—being a medium, in other words—talking to those who have passed away and, most importantly, the upperworld where angels and our Creator live. It was a powerful gift and my saving grace in this battle between good and evil.

A rustling in the bushes stopped me dead in my tracks. I laughed aloud as a black squirrel ran in front of me across O'Brien Manor's cobblestone driveway. I heard, *Lighten up, Paige. Lighten up,* and I was comforted to be home.

CHAPTER TWENTY-ONE

August rolled by rather uneventfully and I was thankful for it. There was no sign of Ariana or her dark magic, no sign of any earthbounds trying to harm my family or me, and no surprises from new evil spirits finding their way to the O'Brien estate. I was riding high as I had buried myself in my studies and ended the July summer school term with an A in calculus class. Dealing with chemistry in the heat of the summer in Mr. Colbert's boring class was almost more than I could bear, but after struggling with it, I managed to receive a solid B+. I looked forward to the awards ceremony coming up in October; I figured it would seem kind of like a graduation to me. I ended up with honours, so I planned to attend the ceremony to celebrate my accomplishment and end this chapter of my life on a positive note.

In the meantime, Dad asked me to help set up his new chiropractic clinic in Camlachie. He was happy the same space he'd rented before Italy was still available. And I was thrilled, as it was located downtown across the street from my favourite restaurant, Magellan's. I figured a father-daughter project would be a good thing, and it would take my mind off the threat of Ariana and her demons. Any work experience would help me in my future career, whatever that would be.

Acting upon the guidance from Uncle Kyle, Grey Owl, and Wayne, I never lost sight of the advice from my supporters and cleansed myself with the grandfather rock by the babbling brook on our estate. Each time I connected with the mystical rock, I felt more and more empowered and peaceful. The added bonus: it was sort of like downloading information from the universe as if being linked to a supercomputer.

On the first day of September, Brad dropped by the manor. I was helping Hanna with the dishes and wiping the last plate as he announced he was heading back to university. Hanna left the kitchen when she heard where the conversation was headed. I carelessly set the plate down with a crash on the kitchen counter and hesitated before replying. I glanced beyond the kitchen nook and stared out the bay window overlooking the rose garden and the forest beyond. I noticed my grandparents' gardens were in need of pruning, as many of the summer blossoms had fallen. Gathering my courage, I wiped the excess water from the speckled navy-and-white granite countertop then turned around to face Brad.

"As I was saying," he said in earnest, "school starts in a couple of days, so I'm heading out in a few hours. I just wanted to come by and congratulate you on finishing high school. How does it feel?"

I gave a weak smile. "It feels like it's about time, I guess."

"Do you have any plans for this year?" he asked as he paced around the kitchen. "I'm going to miss this place ... and you." Brad stared into my eyes. His forlorn look only accentuated his dreamy, dark-brown eyes. The chemistry between us reminded me of why I was attracted to him in the first place. Brad was handsome, but more importantly than that, Brad was a kind soul.

As much as I appreciated Brad's efforts, I knew our star-crossed relationship was long over. And I didn't like being reminded of the fact that my life was put on hold while

Ariana was trying to obtain the Testament and the Seal from my family. I knew Brad wasn't aware of what was going on, but I frowned and shook my head. "My mind has been preoccupied lately. I haven't thought about it really. I'm glad you came by, Brad. I'll tell Grandpa you stopped in to say goodbye. Don't let me keep you."

Brad looked hurt for a moment then managed a smile and said, "Okay, I understand. Well, it was nice seeing you again. Oh and by the way, my mom's attending a quilting festival for a few weeks and then will be on a holiday after that with my Aunt Jo. Just so your family knows."

"Okay, I'll pass it along to my grandparents. Nice seeing you, too," I said softly. "Good luck at school." It was strange to act like we barely knew each other, but I didn't know how else to handle the situation. As much as I wanted to stop Brad from leaving, I knew he couldn't come to grips with the fact that spirits walk amongst us. At least in my family they do.

"Thanks, Paige." Brad turned around to leave, but hesitated. "Oh, and Paige, that girl ... Ariana? She was looking for you. She said something about finding a seal?"

My heart pounded and my face turned beet red. "What? What exactly did she say, Brad? Please. It's important."

Brad shrugged. "Relax a minute. Let me think. I didn't really get what she meant. Like it's an inside joke or something. She said 'tell Paige to bring me the seal, or Trixie gets it.' Who's Trixie anyway?"

It felt like someone punched me in the gut. I had a brief vision of Trixie, kidnapped and restrained in chains. "Brad, I gotta go!" I shouted as I flew out the door to save my friend.

***

When I arrived at the Parkman house, Allan was already there, standing in the front yard in the shade of a mature maple tree. I spied a gash on the side of his face and clutched my stomach for a moment as it became tied up in knots. When I ran closer, I noticed Allan's eyes were swollen and red. Carole arrived behind me, followed by Uncle Kyle and Wayne.

"What's going on?" I asked.

"That girl, she appeared out of nowhere ... from the bushes. Trixie and I were out for a walk. She slashed me with a knife and grabbed Trixie like she was weightless and ran off. I followed her here, but I ... I don't know. I can't explain it. I can't get any closer." Allan's voice cracked. "Why is it always Trixie?"

I hugged Allan because I couldn't think of anything to say to console him. As we broke our embrace, I concentrated on his words. *I can't get any closer. What does he mean?* But as I approached the house, I understood right away; it was as if I'd walked into a soft, padded wall. *Is it surrounding the whole house?* There was no reply. I stood ten feet from the door, unable to reach the steps of the Parkman home.

"What's happening?" I asked as I turned to face Carole and her family. "Is this some sort of spell again?"

"I believe it is. I can feel the dark energy," Wayne said. "Ariana is preventing us from entering. There's a limit to all magic, though. She won't be able to hold this spell forever, will she, Kyle?"

"With our ancestors' help she won't," he replied.

"But how long does Trixie have?" bellowed Allan. "What is happening to my daughter?"

I sensed Trixie's waning energy; she wasn't able to communicate with me in her weakened state.

"Ariana!" I shouted. "Stop! Don't hurt her! Come on out so we can talk!"

The front door burst wide open. Ariana hovered in mid-air once again, sparks shooting from her hands. Her eyes were solid black. She wore the same red cocktail dress she'd been wearing when I saw her on the first day of calculus class. Solid black lines shot up her arms and legs, like strange tattoos. I fought the urge to vomit.

"Ha ha ha. Nice to see you, too, Paige." Her shrill voice was harsh on my ears; I winced and covered them. "I was wondering when you would show up. You took a little longer than I expected."

"What business do you have with Trixie? Let her go!" I pleaded.

"That won't be a problem, Paige. As soon as you give me the Seal of Solomon and the Testament. Then Trixie's all yours." Her piercing cackle sent shivers down my spine.

Allan shifted into his wolf form, Blue-Eyes. He lunged at Ariana but was hurled backwards by the invisible barrier. He leapt to his feet, growling as he went, his incisors bared through curled lips. The reddish hue of his highlights stood out against his grey fur, and his ears were erect, his blue eyes blazing.

"I don't know what you're talking about, Ariana. As if I would know the whereabouts of the Seal of Solomon or his grimoire. You're mad."

"Well, you may not know but your grandfather might. Ask him. Or I'll enjoy torturing Trixie. Tiny knife cuts all over her body. It'll be unbearable for her. She'll bleed out but not before feeling ... every ... single ... cut."

I knew in that moment what I had to do to save Trixie, the friend who had once saved my life.

"I'll be back," I yelled over my shoulder as I transformed into my spirit wolf, Journey, and raced to O'Brien Manor, my creamy coat of fur wind-whipped as I ran. I sensed that my days with my spirit wolf were coming to an end. Perhaps my teacher of balance, loyalty, and spirit protection had been successful; my lessons had been learned. Then I heard a voice.

Remember, Paige, your most powerful weapon has always been inside of you. Your spirit wolf showed you the way and taught you how to protect yourself and your family and sharpened your keen sense of danger. Give thanks for Journey's guidance. Now you are with the eagle, my friend.

I sensed a fatherly energy and could only assume it was my wise, spiritual helper, Wayne.

CHAPTER TWENTY-TWO

Stopping abruptly as I entered the grounds of the O'Brien estate, I transitioned to my human form. And as I ran to the back door, I noticed no light emanating from within the manor, and all windows were closed up tight. A deafening silence surrounded me, and I assumed no one was home.

"Anybody here?" I yelled as I stepped into the kitchen. There was no response. I knew my parents were downtown finishing the last-minute renovations at the clinic. As I rubbed my forehead trying to think of where the rest of my family was, I remembered they were spending the day in town, and Grandpa had an appointment with his doctor.

Not knowing what to do next, I was relieved when a thought pushed into my mind. *Go to the attic. You'll find your answer there.* I raced up the triple-width, black-walnut staircase taking them two steps at a time and didn't stop until I stood below the trapdoor with the pull-down stairs. Without thinking, I unlatched the lock and pulled the stairs towards me. I clambered up the steep steps and into the attic, where I found myself in the middle of the cramped space with Mom's dolls. It had been her favourite childhood place to play. The boy and girl porcelain dolls were seated at the kiddie table, as I called it, and their heads were turned towards each other.

Admiring the ruby necklace placed around the girl's neck, once gifted to Mom on her tenth birthday, I spied a glint of light reflecting off another necklace she held in her hand. I grabbed my chest, as I realized in horror that these dolls were, in fact, made in the likeness of Mackenzie and Conall. *I knew it!* The boy doll wore a goth-style suit and crisp white shirt, like Conall had worn in the first vision I had of him as he lay still, as stiff as a corpse in a coffin. The girl's life-like face resembled Mackenzie's, though she was dressed in more formal clothing. Then I spied the blue ribbon draped across her emerald-green dress. *Can it be true?* And in that light-bulb moment, their mother, Sasha Grace spoke to me.

Their paternal grandfather was a strange man, and he commissioned these dolls in my children's likeness back in our ancestral Scotland. They gave me and their father, Mac, the willies. They found their way here with my mother. She stored them in this attic, hoping they'd be forgotten. And they were ... that is, until we gifted this home to your ancestors, Paige. Your mom discovered the dolls one day and fell in love with them. I believe that's what kept my children here—a supernatural tie to this estate, your mom, and these china dolls. My children remained on this plane instead of returning home through the light. With Mac and me gone, the dolls were the one thing that bound them to this world and reminded them of our family. And to answer one of your questions, when we die most of us do go through the light, and some of us return as guiding angels—spirit guides, as some call us. I am one of your spirit guides, for instance, but you have many. My name was Anne in the mortal realm, but my soul name is Sasha Grace. Now, there's a little bit more information for you. Sasha Grace nodded her head and gave me a knowing smile.

I said aloud, "Such a pretty name, Sasha Grace. Thank you so much for your help. How can I ever thank you? You've done so much for me, saving me from your son Conall, restoring my grandfather's health, and supporting me in my dire time of need. May I ask you one thing?"

Of course, child. What is it?

"What is the necklace the doll resembling Mackenzie holds in her hand?" I turned and pointed to the doll. "I haven't noticed it before. Was this what she carried with her on the day she visited me at my old high school in Scarborough? Was she holding this necklace? Please, I need to know."

Sasha Grace replied, *She was trying to show it to you. It's a ring ... the very signet ring so many are searching for, the Seal of Solomon. She found it one day in the manor, after your grandparents' ancestors moved in. It was stored in a box in your grandfather's closet. He may not have even known he had it in his possession. Bless her heart, she found a silver necklace and attached the ring to it, hoping it would throw the hunters off ... the ones like Ariana who are trying to find it. She was trying to spare you the trouble you've experienced on the estate by bringing the ring to you that day at school. If you'd had the Seal in your hands, none of the hauntings would've happened. You control your family's fate. And humanity's. With the signet ring and its sanctioned supernatural power, which is the key to all of this, no evil can harm you. It is the key to ...*

The voice faded away and I was left alone, yelling the most important question of all time into thin air: "The key to what? Help me, please, Sasha Grace."

I fell to the floor and cried, howling like a wounded animal would. Then I heard it—another wolf's cry in sync with mine. As I stopped to listen, the howl turned into a menacing, guttural growl. My survival instincts kicked into gear as I sensed danger closing in on me.

CHAPTER TWENTY-THREE

A vague memory floated into my consciousness of the day Mackenzie casually mentioned a secret chamber adjacent to the attic. I scrambled to find a hidden trapdoor in the wall. Relieved to find it, I pushed hard and it flashed open. I fell into the secret room, slamming the door shut behind me, leaning breathlessly against it. Vibrations shook the darkened chamber. I gasped as I looked through the glass into the room from which I'd just escaped. A black wolf with wild eyes and a mangy tail looked into my eyes. I broke out into a sweat until it dawned on me. *Wait, he can't see me. If he could, he would have charged through the glass. It's a one-way mirror.*

I slid down the wall, perched on the tips of my toes, and accidentally knocked a tin can off a chair. It made a loud bang as it crashed to the floor. I closed my eyes, expecting the wolf to leap through the mirror at me but, again, nothing happened. *Could it be? A room that has a one-way mirror also has soundproofing? What kind of place is this?*

Calming myself down by using my breathing techniques, I thanked my guiding angels and remained still until the need to find an escape hatch hit me. Crawling, I began to search in the dark, blindly feeling the surface of the walls for my exit. I prayed for a hidden doorway but scared myself when

I knocked something heavy across the room. I scrambled to retrieve it and was relieved to find it was a flashlight. The old fashioned kind with a big box and bulb like an auto's head-light. I flicked it on, overjoyed when the room filled with light. Scanning the room, my eyes widened as I found myself beside two rows of portable wooden chairs, enough to seat twelve, and a pulpit opposite to where I knelt. I approached the pulpit and found a gigantic book, its cover obscured by a thick layer of dust. Searching the lower shelf, I found a cloth and cleaned the cover with methodical, light strokes. I watched in stunned silence as symbols rose from the cover one by one and turned into letters before my very eyes. Then the letters arranged themselves into words, and I discerned the ancient book's title in English: *Testament of Solomon*. I became overwhelmed and light-headed as if the room was spinning. It had to be the original grimoire buried with King Solomon and later recovered by his son, Rehoboam. How could it possibly be here in my ancestors'—the O'Briens and the McDonoughs—secret chamber? The floor shook again and I flicked off the flashlight, slowing my breathing until it was almost undetectable even to me. I was afraid the light might reflect under the secret doorway into the attic or through a random hole in the wall. Worse yet, I feared the wolf would sense me, or, catch my scent.

I focused my thoughts on the sacred grimoire. I had a knowing that this was the one Ariana and every other magic-seeking evil person or demon hunted for. But I had so many questions! I knew the grimoire had been written in Hebrew, perhaps Latin, so why did the title appear in English for me? *Who is helping me? My spirit guides? My guardian angel, Sasha Grace, perhaps?*

Not really expecting an answer, I peered through the mirror and watched as my predator stealthily examined every nook and cranny of the attic. It seemed like he searched for hours until, finally, the wolf shapeshifted into none other than Beelzebul, with his black, behemoth, shadowy form, and flaming red eyes. I knew he couldn't see the signet ring held in Mackenzie's hand because he wasn't a pure soul, but I wondered why he couldn't see me or sense I was close by. I became increasingly aware of a nine-foot-high force field that surrounded me. *Is this what Peggy eluded to about our auras and our own soul protection?*

I picked up the grimoire and clasped it to my chest, amazed to be the keeper of such an important historical artifact. I didn't need to understand it, but I knew in my heart I had to protect it with my mind, body, and soul, even risk my life to ensure it remained hidden for many, many, more centuries to come. It was, after all, my destiny. Game on!

CHAPTER TWENTY-FOUR

I heard a faint voice calling my name but I continued to wander, lost in a garden with low-lying fog blanketing my view of the ground I walked upon. There were three-foot shrubs and over-grown vines covering a white trellis full of blossoming purple clematis flowers, a white birdbath decorated with violet hummingbirds, and Japanese maple trees with purple leaves. I meandered aimlessly, not knowing if someone was about to meet me in this beautiful location or if my soul had travelled to Heaven. I found a white bench and sat down to appreciate the beauty surrounding me. Suddenly, the grimoire materialized next to me. I waited for someone to appear, but no one did. I picked up the Testament of Solomon and opened it to the first page. There was a written list of protocols for protecting oneself before even considering performing a magic spell. I wondered why I was able to read the text, knowing now it was written in Hebrew. Perhaps I was in a magical land where magical things happened, like in the secret chamber room. There was so much information to cover. I read it at ten times the pace I would normally read, and I was known for being a fast reader.

Digesting the information seemed easy enough as I glanced around periodically to enjoy my beautiful surroundings. A monarch butterfly with orange and black wings flew by before returning to sit on my left hand. I lovingly admired it, thanking it for keeping me company, as if it was a person. After a time, the butterfly flew away.

I began to read from the Testament of Solomon again, and this time I landed on the page that held the key to controlling demons. It had a warning: the spell could only be recited by those with pureness of heart. And I wondered, do I really possess this quality or would I find out the hard way if I read the incantation out loud?

On that thought, I heard these words:

Only the Chosen One would do these things: save her grand-father from his impending death at the hands of Conall; risk her life in the cemetery to uncover the mystery of the tablet; be called upon to help Dexter at his end-of-life time after he tried many times to kill you; help to save Carole from the wolf, carrying her up the ridge to the dilapidated cottage, despite bleeding profusely from your own tragic wounds, and leading her out of the cottage to safety through the darkened cemetery on Halloween; stay behind on the estate with your grandparents to help look after them; and to bear responsibility for Trixie, Dexter, and Delia's black lab who happens to be Allan's long lost stepdaughter, Trixie! And instead of involving your parents, you spared them the knowledge of the evil haunting O'Brien Manor. Need we remind you any further of the pureness of heart you have shown and proven to our Almighty Father? Every time you are put in grave danger, Paige Alexandra Maddison, you put the other person's needs ahead of your own. You have spared your friend Bradley Adam Parkman from ever knowing the truth of the evil still walking the grounds of the estate, and in his home. You followed your guidance from the upperworld and kept secrets from those you love, in the name of love. You spared them the agony and torture of knowing the truth. It is not their journey, after all.

We know it's a lonely path for you but we are always here sup-porting you, and you have many friends too. You, Paige, are the key to ending the final battle against the evil that has afflicted your family for centuries. Ariana's mother uncovered the history of the location of the Testament of Solomon using magic and tracked it to your family. It has been guarded, stolen, returned to its original ancestry, stolen again, and so it goes on. Your family has been charged with guarding the Testament and the signet ring because you and your ancestors have proven your worthiness time and time again; you guard it as if it's your own, without snooping into its content. You were urged to read the spell, the one where the words lifted off the page, and it is now recorded in your soul's memory. It will help you in your final battle against Ariana and Beelzebul. Don't be afraid, child. You will have many soldiers by your side. But do not forget, you are the one to end it all. Our Almighty Father has sanctioned it.

***

Snapping awake, I clutched my chest and remembered I held the *Testament of Solomon* in my arms. *Oh, thank goodness no one's found me.* I placed the huge book back on its stand and slid the cloth over the cover. Glancing around the room, I sensed I stood in the middle of a secret chamber my ancestors had once gathered in, probably Conall and Mackenzie's ancestors too. They must have held private rituals here and secured their much-needed protection from the evil lurking around them. It was a sanctuary of sorts.

I noticed a break in the woodwork. My heart skipped a beat. *Could it be my escape route?* Darting over, I felt the outline of a secret door. I instinctively knew it was a trapdoor similar to the one I had entered the room through and knew if I pushed hard on it, the door would open. And it did. A narrow, spiral staircase appeared before me and my heart raced. Yet another secret at O'Brien Manor.

I navigated down the circular stairway until I reached a landing with a long and skinny hallway. There was only one way to turn, so I marched ahead until I met what I presumed to be a false wall — the exit door — half the length of a standard door. I pushed on it, but the door wouldn't open. The flashlight revealed a small, brass latch and I unhinged it. I tumbled onto the landing that overlooked O'Brien Manor's foyer with its beautiful white marble flooring. I remembered the first day I stumbled upon this jaw-dropping sight ... the foyer when we moved to Camlachie from Scarborough, or what mom fondly referred to as 'Scarberia', whatever we wanted to call it. I felt a pang of homesickness for my old friends and teachers, but it was quickly followed by a sense of duty and a knowing. The day I first walked through the oversize mahogany double doors was the beginning of my destiny to save my family and all of humanity from evil. *The signet ring and the grimoire are in safe keeping. There is no time to waste.*

Racing back to Brad's home, my mind was focussed on the horrible truth that Beelzebul could shapeshift into whatever form he wished. He was so close to catching me yet he couldn't sense me. *What is this power that I now possess?* I felt invincible. My soul and aura had somehow sprung into protection mode like a force field, hiding me like an invisible cloak. I didn't understand it, but I knew better than to question it. In the time it took to reach Allan, Carole, Uncle Kyle, and Wayne, I was transformed into a different person, an empowered, seventeen-year-old female warrior.

"Is Trixie still trapped inside?" I asked Allan and Carole as I reached Brad's house. Allan stood shaking. He looked sad and confused and frustrated all at the same time. I knew Carole was trying to maintain her composure, to comfort Allan and assure him everything would be all right, but she seemed concerned as well.

"Yup. There's been no sound, nothing," Allan replied, his voice trembling. "I'm going out of my mind, Paige. Please help her. We don't know what's happening to my poor daughter." Allan slumped to his knees, his hands on his head. "What have I done? I should've been here for her. This is the third time I've failed her. I wasn't there for her when her mother died, or when she was bullied by the wolves in Granite's pack, and now ... There's no telling what Ariana's doing to my daughter, my Trixie."

I placed my hand on his shoulder and Allan jerked backwards. "Yeeeowwwww! What was that, a lightning bolt? That hurts!" He pulled away and rubbed his shoulder.

"Sorry, Allan. I've been through sort of a ... well, a mini-course on how to protect us from the darkness. Oh never mind. We don't have time for this right now."

Carole interrupted. "What are we going to do, Paige? Time is running out. Wait, where did my dad and Uncle Kyle go?"

"They said something about consulting your ancestors," Allan said. "I think they went to your cabin."

"Make no mistake. They are gathering reinforcements to help Trixie," said Carole.

"I know. And I'm grateful. Having your family on our team is a saving grace."

"That's right, Allan. For now, we are three strong. And we are going to save your daughter," I said. We stood side by each and I felt the strength emanating from my friends. With their help, I could accomplish anything.

"Ariana, can you come out?" It was seconds before she appeared on the front porch and hovered there, just glaring at us with her crazed eyes. Though it made me shiver for a moment, I continued.

"So, Ariana. What's your plan? I guess you don't have the grimoire — you know the one, the original one of King Solomon's — after all."

Ariana shrieked. She flew back and forth across the porch like she was pacing. "How do you know, Paige? Aha, you found the original, did you? Well, you just gave away your family secret. Get it for me or Trixie dies."

Ariana disappeared for a moment and reappeared with Trixie. The two of them were firmly planted on the ground, and Ariana held a knife to Trixie's neck. I watched in horror as a crimson ribbon of blood trickled down Trixie's arm, dripped from her fingers, and splattered at her feet. I swallowed the urge to vomit. This stand-off had to end.

"Prohibere!" I held up my right hand, and as I did, my energy blasted through Ariana's invisible shield and knocked her over backwards. I yelled, "Go, Allan! Save your daughter!"

Allan ran like the spirit wolf he was inside and swept Trixie into his arms. Together, they escaped into the woods. I remained behind with Carole to face Ariana.

"Since when do you speak Latin, Paige? H-how d-d-did you d-do that?" Ariana said, a confused look on her face. "You don't practice magic. What happened? Who are you?"

"Look, Ariana, you don't have to do this. Live from a place of love. Remember love is what's most important." Frustrated by her lack of emotion or response, I continued. "Let's just say I got in touch with my ancestry and a few guiding friends." I took a step towards her, and Ariana took a step back.

"This isn't over, Paige," she shrieked. She ran inside the house and slammed the door behind her.

"Well, that's it then, at least for now," said Carole. "If you don't mind me asking, Paige, what happened to you? You seem different."

"I had a moment with the grimoire. You know, the *Testament of Solomon* that Ariana is looking for. And somehow I picked up some Latin. But let me say this, Carole. Visiting your home ... meeting your dad ... your land ... your grandfather rock was instrumental in my spiritual evolvement. If I hadn't done that first, I don't think I'd be able to connect to the grimoire. Spiritual cleansing was definitely needed, and I'm grateful to you. Thank you so much." I gave her a bear hug. "You released me from the bonds of negative energy. Thanks to Jewish history and precious artifacts, I will never again underestimate the power of Celtic and First Nations ancestry. It seems we're all connected somehow by the belief in our Creator and in the power of love ... and a bit of divine intervention," I admitted to Carole. "And I am forever grateful for our upperworld supporters, our angels, and our God."

"Hallelujah to that," Carole added and high-fived me.

CHAPTER TWENTY-FIVE

After the showdown with Ariana at the Parkman's home, I felt confident about my abilities and ready to defeat the evil on the O'Brien estate. I had a knowing that it was up to me to visit the chamber room, without consulting anyone in my family, and to absorb the knowledge of the *Testament of Solomon*. The grimoire called to me at nights, mostly. I began to feel like a spy, leading a double life. I helped my dad paint his new clinic during the day. We enjoyed a few lunches at Magellan's. And I made sure I spent equal time with Mom, my grandparents, and Hanna. In fact, I helped them can pickles for the upcoming winter months. It was a gruelling task but I wasn't going to complain. I rather enjoyed the process with my family, together, safe and sound.

"Paige, did you know that Cleopatra, the last reigning pharaoh of Egypt, loved pickles? Apparently it goes back centuries, this need to make the best sour pickles. You are a fearless fermenter, dear. Thanks for finding the secret ingredients — the kosher salt and the pièce de résistance, the tannin-rich grape leaves from the wild crop on Carole's property. It will be the ticket to our success this year. Your grandpa and I love crunchy dills. No more soft pickles or hollow ones again for us. What a peach you are." Grandma practically sang as she poured compliments over me. I revelled in the moment. "And thank you too, Lori. You've spared your dad and me from much of the physical labour. Thank you for attending to the dreaded, steamy-hot cannery pot."

"I rather enjoy the role of stirring the pot. Kind of like 'double, double, toil and trouble.'" Mom made a twitchy-looking face and screwed up her nose. She looked adorable. Laughing she said, "No, seriously, it's no trouble at all, Mom. I enjoy our time together. We were in Italy for quite awhile. It's good to be home again." Mom smiled and gave Grandma a kiss on her cheek. Out of the blue, she asked, "So, Paige. Are you going to send in the application forms for university? For January?"

I had no idea how we got from pickles to university applications. "Actually, I forgot to fill them in. They're on my dresser. I've decided to apply to the University of Toronto and McGill in Montreal. They're tops."

"Wait a minute. We live sixty-five miles from London, to Western University. Why not there? Then we can pop in to see you, dear," Mom said. "Maybe even take you out for dinner."

"And *that's* the reason I'm not applying there." I laughed as if I hadn't a care in the world. It was great to have a knowing that all would be resolved upon the O'Brien estate, for all our sakes, and to forget the pressure for a moment. "I just know you and Dad can't control yourselves and would show up unannounced."

"Oh, fiddle-de-dee, Paige. Your grandpa and I would love it too. Can't you give it a thought?" asked Grandma. She looked so sweet with her tight, curly, red hair.

Laughing at her funny expression, I said, "Nope, sorry Grandma. I think by the time I'm ready to leave for school, I might want to put some distance between Camlachie and me. No offense."

"We understand, Paige. It's only natural for you to want to spread your wings," added Grandpa. "Wherever you choose to go, they'll be lucky to have you. We only hope that you'll want to come home for holidays, at least."

"Thanks, Grandpa. Of course. Well, if that's all for now, I'll go fill in those forms. Thanks for today, by the way. I really enjoyed helping out. I can't wait to try those pickles."

"Don't worry, we'll send some away with you when the time comes. It takes a few months for them to become crunchy dills," said Grandma.

As I walked along the hallway to my bedroom, I chuckled as I recalled the story Mom once told me about the ongoing argument she had with Grandpa over the number of rooms in O'Brien Manor. Seems Grandpa was right all along. There were indeed sixty-three rooms, as he had stated time and again. Note to self: *Don't confirm the number with Mom or she'll storm upstairs to find the secret chamber room. At least not for now.*

As I hesitated outside my bedroom door, it warmed my heart to listen to the happy chatter echoing down the hallway from the kitchen. I smiled knowing soon all would be resolved on the O'Brien estate. With a little help from my friends and supernatural guides nothing was impossible.

CHAPTER TWENTY-SIX

Halloween loomed. I knew I had to be ready for it; periodic drumming reminded me to return to the brook to perform my cleansings in preparation of what was to come. The brook was my private sanctuary on the haunted estate, and I was grateful for it. There was an energy in the air that increased daily. We all sensed it. Carole notified me that her dad and uncle were on high alert. Prayers, cleansing ceremonies, and mindfulness were their defences against the brewing evil.

Trixie recovered from Ariana's torment, with the help of her dad. For now, my relationship with Allan remained stalled. Nothing was more important than what we had to face and conquer. We both feared Ariana would threaten Trixie again. Nerves aside, after all I had been through I was ready to end the battle with Ariana, between good and evil, once and for all. I felt it right down to my soul. What better time than on Halloween when the liminal veil grew thin? Though many talked about the evil spirits that walked this good earth on Halloween, I believed that many good spirits did too. But Grandpa mentioned a dreaded black moon would occur near All Hallows' Eve, and we would need all the help we could get this Halloween. They say there's safety in numbers, and I for one wanted to believe it.

Without any knowledge of what a black moon was, I hit the internet and searched link after link until I began to understand what we were up against. The black moon, the second new moon within the month, enables any magic performed during that time to have extra-special powers. Most people didn't notice the new moon, especially because of its darkened state; to those who practiced magic, they counted down the days on their calendars to this powerful event. That realization made me and my friends uneasy.

I found myself lost in thought often, wondering if the final showdown would be just between Ariana and me, or if something much more ominous was in store. Much to my surprise, I had no visions or predictions about it. But I had a knowing in my heart, in every fibre of my being, that this was the fight of the century. Many believed an apocalypse would be the end of the old world order and the beginning of the new, but if my communications with the upperworld were accurate, the showdown would happen on the O'Brien estate and most of humanity would be none the wiser. Carole, Allan, Trixie, Peggy and all of our ancestors were the watchers protecting the world order. And I was ready for what was to come. A sense of knowing in my mind, body, and soul allowed me to foresee that failure was not an option.

I was drawn more and more to the 63rd room, the secret chamber, and often climbed through the invisible half-door located on the landing of the black-walnut staircase, camouflaged by rose-coloured wallpaper. I pushed a letter opener through the break in the wall, unlocking the brass latch, and crawled through the second floor entryway, up the circular stairwell, and into O'Brien Manor's sacred space. I had collected a few candles and lit them while I read from the Testament. It was particularly captivating at night. During this process, my surroundings disappeared and I was catapulted to the white, rectangular room with the table and chairs where I had once visited with the man in the floor-length white robe. I felt protected and invisible while study-ing from this mystical grimoire. My long, curly, auburn hair began to grow a white streak on the right side of my head, as if reading and processing the words of the Testament produced a physical reaction to the spiritual transformation I was undergoing. No one seemed to mention it and I was relieved about that.

Each night, while lying in bed, I was reminded to say my protection prayers and the prayer for the lost souls. I thought back to the year before when I had transitioned a football-stadium-size room full of lost souls. It motivated me to pray harder, repeating my two special prayers — Psalm 23 and The Lord's Prayer — and in my mind's eye, as I opened the tunnel towards the light, I prayed, *Dear God, I am praying for the lost souls that walk this earth to transition through the white light for the goodness of humankind, and for the goodness of themselves.*

I felt empathy for them, as many were trapped here in our plane and they had forgotten how to return home. Some were trapped by their well-meaning relatives who couldn't seem to let them go. Some poor souls died traumatically, like in a car accident, and couldn't believe they were dead. And others were so attached to their material possessions, their home, that they refused to leave. When the new owners moved into the house, they were subjected to attacks from their acquired earthbound. Doors slammed shut, coasters moved, keys disappeared then reappeared. It was a process of letting go for those who died and for those who were left behind. Yet, in my heart I felt some souls remained in our plane to help their loved ones, as Mackenzie had, to keep her brother, Conall, company.

***

One day, I heard drumming, low at first, then increasing in volume and intensity until it amounted to a crescendo, much like surround sound. I knew I had to return to Carole's house and visit with her dad. I ran past Peggy's cottage and around the side of her house to the wood chip path. I felt a runner's high by the time I reached Carole's land. I carefully retrieved a small tobacco pouch I'd bought in town, struck a wooden match and lit it on fire, and watched as the flames burned out. I chanted the prayer Carole had taught me, and when I arrived at the cabin, I pounded on the door. There was no answer. As I stood there, frustrated, I heard a whisper.

Welcome, Paige. Please come to the grandfather rock.

Without hesitation, I turned on my heels and ran towards the healing place. When I arrived, I knelt down, prayed, and gathered myself. I did my deep breathing and then placed my left hand on the grandfather rock.

Paige, you are the Chosen One to help our people, our land, your family. Listen to your heart and your inner wisdom. This is what will help you most in the fight against the evil. You already have the answers you need, but know this — we are here support-ing you. We will be with you on the day it begins.

A vision of the wise old man entered my consciousness. Telepathically, I answered, *Thank you, oh Wise One. I can see you now in my mind's eye, like before, with your white braids and feather, and wise, weathered face. Your love and support is in my heart. Thank you so much for helping me.*

Though no reply came, I watched as the wise man nodded and faded away. It was reassuring to know that my First Nations ancestors would be by my side during the troubled times ahead. It was incredible for me to know we shared the same belief; we are all connected as one.

***

Four days before Halloween, I felt an urgency to step up my prayers and to safeguard the signet ring. I often sat in the attic, guarding the Seal of Solomon attached to the necklace, reminding myself to never place it upon my finger. I knew in my heart it was not my place to wear such a powerful talisman, one of humankind's most sought-after treasures. Many archaeologists, scientists, religious cults, demons, and amateur witches hunted for the Seal of Solomon. It still shocked me that my family held the key to humanity's survival. The majority of hunters thought it was stored in a vault in the Vatican. But that didn't make any sense at all. The Vatican would be subjected to thievery and put in harm's way. I began to understand why it was placed in the O'Briens' charge. After all, in the course of history, who were we but an invisible footprint?

I was warned by a soft voice.

Thank you for your prayers for the lost souls. You have completed your promise. Now you must gather your energy to preserve your inner power. Remember, Paige, live from a place of love. It conquers all that is evil.

I fell into a deep sleep and was jolted awake to find 11:11 flashing on my alarm clock. I forgot for a moment what day it was and then I remembered, it was Devil's Night, the night before Halloween.

Frantically dressing, I stormed into the kitchen and found a note on the breakfast nook table. It read, *Paige, we are gathering firewood for All Hallows' Eve. You remember ... the hallow fire. Your breakfast is in the refrigerator, fit for a hero. You'll see. Just microwave it, dear. Love, Hanna xo*

Why not eat something? I thought, still feeling a bit out of sorts. I laughed as I retrieved the heavy tray from the fridge and slid it on the counter. I eyed the heap of pancakes, strawberries, and sausage. *Hanna must think my friends are stopping by!* I fixed a plate for myself and popped it in the microwave.

As I waited, I heard the front door knocker. It echoed through the foyer into the kitchen. I hurried to answer it and was thrilled to see Carole, Uncle Kyle, and Wayne — my First Nations family.

"Fantastic! Wait 'til you see the breakfast of champions made for us," I said.

As Wayne crossed the threshold into O'Brien Manor, he asked, "Are you ready for tonight, Paige?"

"Believe it or not, I just got up. I don't know how I feel, but I think I'm rested. I was just about to eat. Would you like some?"

"Well, that's why we're here. Your grandma rang Peggy, who rang us, and invited us for a hungry man's breakfast, as she described it," Uncle Kyle said with a chuckle.

"Please, come into the kitchen," I insisted, waving my arm and pointing the way.

"Well, today's the day we've all been waiting for. Can you feel it, Paige?" asked Uncle Kyle as we gathered around the kitchen island.

"You mean the heightened energy that won't stop encircling me?" I asked.

"Yes, we're all sensing it," added Carole. She rolled her eyes. "Here we go, another Halloween with Paige Alexandra Maddison. Beware everyone. Last year we were tormented and ended up at the dilapidated cottage trapped by none other than the family friend, Dexter. He was possessed and tried to kill Paige and me. Bradford was a real charmer. And oh, let's not forget our fifty or so wolf friends semi-protecting us." Her laugh had a nervous edge to it, but it was great to hear her attempt some lightheartedness.

"I know, Carole. I agree it was a spine-chilling night. But we've learned so much over this past year. About our spirituality ... who our real friends are. And we know the upperworld has our backs. I have no fear whatsoever today." And on that admission, even I was shocked. "And I'm grateful for the support of all of you—"

"Good thing, then," said Wayne, laughing as he slapped Uncle Kyle's back. "I told you our girl Paige had it all under control."

I retrieved the warriors' breakfast from the microwave and passed it to Uncle Kyle and made a plate of food for each of us. We stood at the kitchen island and hastily ate some sausage and pancakes ignoring the strawberries. Sustenance was needed.

Between bites, I said, "I've said my protection prayers. I've cleansed myself at the brook—at your home, too—and my guiding angels have said they are here no matter what. Oh, and don't forget the two sentinels guarding me."

"Pardon me, two what?" asked Wayne as he set his fork down.

"Two sentinels. You know, white dogs. They'll call for the archangels if I can't voice it or send a telepathic message myself. The archangels promised to answer their call."

Wayne's eyes widened, as did Uncle Kyle's. "I'm so relieved to hear this, Paige. White dogs, in our culture, represent our Creator, and His magic is bestowed upon them. They are great protectors and represent purity and a sense of renewal. You might say you have a pipeline to our Creator with no obstacles or spiritual blocks in the way. I'm relieved to hear this," Wayne said. He slapped Uncle Kyle on the shoulder, again.

"Yes, we're relieved," Uncle Kyle added while studying Wayne's face. "Paige, this is much more than we feared. But now our warrior selves are on high alert. No fear, no negativity. We go into this battle with love and our soldiers' arsenal."

"Thanks for the breakfast, Paige. We must go now and prepare for tonight. We'll return when summoned," Wayne said.

I watched as my three First Nations friends exited the manor. They were my protectors, my family, and my saviours. We shall soldier on, together.

I retreated after my heavy breakfast to lay on my antique daybed and awoke to a nudging, much like someone pushing on my shoulder. I was stunned as three o'clock flashed on my alarm clock. As I changed into my purple yoga outfit, my mind raced with thoughts of what was to come. I ascended the triple-width black walnut staircase, slid an envelope opener up the side of the trapdoor, and unlatched the lock. As I started up the spiral staircase, whispers echoed around me and followed me into the secret chamber room. Low at first, the whispers grew louder.

Paige, Paige. I know you've found the ring and the grimoire. I'm coming for you. Either bring them to me or I'll bring wretchedness upon your home and everyone in it.

Gales of morbid laughter like that of the wicked witch from *The Wizard of Oz* echoed around the room. Ringing in my ears overwhelmed me. I jammed the palms of my hands over my ears to stop it, to stop her. I recognized Ariana's voice calling out to me. She was a sick and twisted sister, all right. The old Paige would've been intimidated; the new Paige needed the battle to begin. My soul cried out for it, the need for my destiny, to fight Ariana and whoever joined her, to finally begin.

After studying the grimoire one last time, I carefully placed it upon the pulpit and hid it under the cloth. A whisper commanded, *Retrieve the Seal of Solomon.* I crawled through the trapdoor into the attic, grabbed the necklace with the Seal, and placed it around my neck. Somehow, with no memory of how I got there, I found myself standing on the second floor landing. A flashback to the first time Mom brought me to her favourite childhood hangout crossed my mind. I relaxed while thinking of her and the advice she once gave to me: Peggy is your mentor; she was mine, too. The memory prompted me to visit my trusted friend.

I telepathically asked Peggy, *May I come for a visit now before Devil's Night begins?* She replied, *Yes, hurry.* In a flash, I arrived at Peggy's Victorian-style screen door, I was happy to see her welcome me inside.

"Paige! Thank you for coming. I needed to see you. I understand you've been doing your protection prayers. And now you must do your cleansing in the shower by saying the Lord's Prayer, Psalm 23, and then the cleansing prayer. Can you remember to do this, child?" she asked.

"I promise, I will," I answered. "But fear not, Peggy. Rest assured, we will win. Somehow, I know we will."

"Great to hear the confidence in your voice, Paige. It's most important that you go into this fight with love in your heart and your soul protected. We don't want Ariana blindsiding you with one of her spells. And we really don't know who's teamed up with her."

"I have an idea, and his name is Beelzebul."

"Hush, child. Never say his name out loud. It invites him in. Clear your mind, now."

"Okay, black-eyed Susans and lavender thoughts it is." I smiled at Peggy and noticed a frown on her face. "Don't worry, Peggy. I'm taking this very seriously. I have spent time with the *Testament of Solomon* and have guarded the Seal, too. There is only one outcome, our victory, tonight."

Peggy hugged me for dear life and sent me on my way. As I ran down the gravel road to the O'Brien estate, I heard her say, *Shine your light, Paige. Shine your light. People have been trying to shut it down since the day you were born.*

I will, indeed, Peggy. Thanks to you, I replied in kind. Then I was off to cleanse myself. How could I battle evil if I did not ensure evil was not attached to me or to my soul?

In preparation for the All Hallows' Eve battle, I jumped in the shower and recited, as suggested, *Dear God, please cleanse, clear, fill, and encapsulate me with the white Christ-light of healing and protection. Please take all evil energies or entities away from me, to their proper plane, and close my aura so that they may not return. Please replace them with higher, stronger, more powerful vibrations.* I inhaled a long, deep breath and exhaled the negative energies collected in my aura, repeating this several times.

I spent the remainder of Devil's Night in the 63rd room. Guided by my protectors to remain isolated from any negative energy building upon the estate, I concentrated on positive thoughts, studying the Testament and gathering my strength for tomorrow's events. Grandpa's birthday celebration this Halloween would have to wait until the battle was won.

That night as I snuck into my cosy bed, I was happy to hear Mom's laughter, followed by footsteps towards my room. As she entered, she plopped on the bed and said, "Paige, we've missed you today. Everything okay, dear?"

"Of course, Mom," I replied, as I reached up to hug her. I wanted to spare her the sordid details of events yet to come, so I tried to change the subject. "Oh, did I tell you that Madame Clouthier, my French teacher, is an old friend of yours? And she wants to go out to lunch with you sometime."

"I forgot she came back to teach. Thanks, Paige. I'll make a note of that and reach out to her. Look, I know you're going through something, but my instincts are guiding me to leave you be. You've got this, Paige. Whatever it is you're going through, I believe in you. You can handle it. You're an O'Brien and a Maddison, after all." She ran her fingers through my hair and tucked it behind my right ear. "Whatever's going on, if I can help you in any way … just ask."

"Thanks, Mom. You and Dad are the best parents ever. I love you both so much," I said.

"There, there, Paige. It's okay. Everything will be fine. I know Halloween is a rough time for our family. But with all of us doing our prayers, well, it connects our energies as one. We can fight whatever comes our way when the liminal veil thins."

I sat back and stared into her soulful eyes. "Thanks, Mom. That's exactly what I needed to hear from you. Does Dad pray?" I asked.

"Believe it or not, he does, nightly. He prays for our souls. Well, nighty-night then. Sweet dreams." Mom kissed me on the forehead and pulled my covers up to my neck. "Sleep peacefully, Paige. We're all in this together."

"Night, Mom. And thanks for stopping in to check on me. Say good night to Dad too, please."

"What's this? Of course I want to say good night to our favourite daughter," Dad added as he entered my room. "I wouldn't miss it, especially on Devil's Night. I pray for us all, Paige. Our family is three strong, now six strong with Hanna and your grandparents, and with Peggy, and Carole's family, and Allan and Trixie ... well, our tribe has certainly grown hasn't it?" His sweet smile and twinkling blue eyes relaxed me as they always did.

"It sure has. Oh, and Dad, did I tell you I played that drum solo I created back in Scarborough for my music final? You remember the one?"

"Well, isn't that terrific! I bet they loved it. Wish I'd been there to see you play, Paige. I'm glad we're home now. We've missed you so."

"I love you both for eternity," I said. Then I rolled on my side to sleep.

"We love you, Paige, to the sky and back, to the sky and back, to infinity and beyond. Good night, dear," my parents said simultaneously.

The click of the light switch was the last thing I remembered until I awoke the next day.

CHAPTER TWENTY-SEVEN

Before dawn broke, I crept up to the secret chamber room one last time. I brought snacks that I knew would give me lots of energy on this hell-raising day. Nuts with coconut pieces, beef jerky, dried dates, and carrots would have to sustain me. I absorbed as much of the *Testament of Solomon* as I could endure, which took me most of the day amidst some cat naps. Finally, I felt ready and consulted my cell phone. It flashed five o'clock, which meant the witching hour would soon begin. As if in a trance, I returned to my room. The manor was still. I knew my family would be outside tending to the hallow fire.

Cleansing was best performed when alone and no other energy was near. I said my prayers in the shower to rid myself of any negative energy I may have acquired in my sleep. Then I dressed in my black skinny jeans, an indigo, long-sleeve T-shirt, and my army boots, and grabbed the angel Dexter had once gifted to me, placing her in my back jean pocket. Next, I put on a sterling silver cross necklace I'd found in the night table next to my bed. It hung draped overtop of the Seal ... almost cloaking its existence.

Grabbing my black leather jacket and gloves, I marched out the east side of the estate towards Brad's house. I heard,

Godspeed, Paige. I am with you in spirit tonight, followed by heartfelt warmth. I knew it was Peggy's blessing and a royal send off for me. I sent a reply, *Thank you.*

Okay, Ariana, here I come.

Allan and Trixie joined me on the O'Brien estate path to the Parkman's property, as did Uncle Kyle and Wayne, too. We all leapt forward into our spirit wolf forms. And I was relieved to see the hellhounds had joined our ranks. They were protecting the order of their world, too.

We arrived at the house fifty or sixty strong. There was no one to be seen, no one I could sense. *I couldn't be wrong, could I?* Ariana's stronghold was at Sarah's house. And then it dawned on me—the cemetery! Perfect! It's where I'd solved the mystery of the stone tablet—the key to escaping the dilapidated cottage when evil Dexter hunted Carole and me—and the sacred place where Sasha Grace had first appeared. It would be the strongest, spiritual epicentre on the estate for my friends and me to make our last stand, united as one, against the evil gathered there. And I hoped my ancestors buried there might help, too. Mortal Ariana would not have access to this knowledge of my history on the O'Brien estate. And then, it hit me. *Where's Carole?*

I howled out the instructions for everyone to run to the O'Brien cemetery. My heart pounded, as I could not sense Carole. We galloped as fast as we could. There, perched on the angel statue, was Beelzebul in his daunting shadowy form. When he spied us, he nodded to Ariana who shapeshifted into her witch-like form and hovered in mid-air. Blue-Eyes and I transformed into our human form.

"Bring me the ring, Paige, and the Testament, or your friend will die today. Look over yonder." She cast a fiery red light over the cemetery as the sunlight retreated.

My stomach flipped as I spied Carole strung up in a tree, straining to maintain her footing on a feeble branch to prevent falling and being hung by her neck. I stumbled for a moment and gazed up to the blackened, stormy sky. Glancing towards Wayne and Uncle Kyle who stood frozen in place, it unnerved me to see the veins in their forehead popped out, mouths agape. We had our answer to Carole's whereabouts. *How could we have missed this?*

"Stop it, Ariana." Again, I raised my right hand and pushed a ball of energy at her, knocking her down. She landed with a loud thud amongst the tombstones. I ignored the legion of demons bringing up the rear. The nasty, ugly creatures that crawled out of the darkness. Beelzebul flew towards me and again I raised my right hand, casting energy towards him. It only slowed him down for a few seconds. Beelzebul fought back, shapeshifting into the red dragon with his scaly skin and sharp talons, blazing red eyes, and outstretched wings the size of Archangel Michael's. I gulped but fearlessly aimed my right hand at him again, and energy flowed through my body. It was a relief to see the dragon fly backwards as if pushed by my propulsive force. I noticed the Archangels Michael and Raphael standing united behind me, as was Gabriel, and together their energies cast a bright, white light. All of my spirit wolf friends had shapeshifted into their human forms, and the hellhounds were mighty fierce, growling through bared teeth dripping with saliva. I had enlisted an army to help me fight this final battle, but I knew in my heart I needed more help.

"I call upon God. In the name of our Heavenly Father, please help us here today to rid our earthly plane of the devil and his helpers." I recited Psalm 23 and then continued. "Please help us defeat the enemy here before us and help us to save my best friend, Carole. Take the enemy away; they do not belong here." I made the sign of the cross on my chest.

Once again, Beelzebul flew towards me. A bright, white light enveloped me, and I drew comfort from Archangel

Michael as he stepped up to shield our army with an invisible force field.

"That's far enough, Beelzebul," Archangel Michael announced. "We've waited patiently to get you out in the open, my once trusted friend, turned foe. It has taken a century to put this together—the right people, the right spirits, the right souls, the right time. Imagine! A seventeen-year-old mortal will be your undoing. It is sanctioned."

Suddenly urged and without hesitation, I ripped Mackenzie's necklace from my neck and placed the Seal of Solomon in the palm of my left hand, my receiving hand, sending shockwaves through my entire body, knowing that I'd be protected from any evil spirits or spells. My soul arose from my body and spoke telepathically to my oppressor. Only the good spirits from the light could help me speak the incantation I had learned in the magical garden. I slammed back into my body and held up my right hand. I gave a continuous blast of energy from deep within my soul, so intense that its massive fireball knocked Beelzebul into the legions of a fiery cavern, and we watched as he was swallowed up, trapped inside. His blazing red eyes faded, and I watched as his wings and body burst into flames. Soon, his carcass disintegrated; ashes to ashes, dust to dust. All that remained was a blackened hole in the ground, his soul was trapped forever.

I dropped to the ground from exhaustion. The cheering from my compatriots rang out through the cemetery. Shocked by what had happened, I stared at my hands and wondered where the energy had come from.

I was barely conscious of Wayne rescuing his daughter, cutting her down from the tree. He carried her in his arms and laid her on the ground next to me. I wrapped her in my arms. "Oh thank goodness you're okay!" I said as tears poured forth.

"It's okay, Paige. Ariana's not as tough as she thinks. You were right. Please, go to her," insisted Carole.

I shook my head and whispered, "Wait, what are you saying?"

Help her.

I raised my right hand without realizing what I was doing and turned my energy on Ariana in a bout of anger. She had kidnapped and threatened to kill my best friend in the world.

"Stop, Paige! You'll kill her," commanded Archangel Michael. "Harness your power. Bring it back into you. Control it. Remember what our Almighty Father said to you. Remember, Paige!"

And it dawned on me. I pulled the powerful energy back into me, tingling surged throughout my body, and I let it loose, releasing it into the universe. Fiery orange energy beamed upwards from me and lit up the sky. As I stepped back, my inner voice issued a familiar command, *Live from a place of love. It conquers all that is evil.* I ran over to Ariana and picked up her lifeless body.

"Where are you taking her?" asked Carole as she jumped up. "I want to come with you."

"To your land, if you don't mind. I think the grandfather rock can help her."

"Dad, do you think it'll help?" asked Carole.

"Yes, you go, too, Carole. Be her witness. Go now, honey," Wayne said. "It'll be fine. Our ancestors await."

We ran as fast as our legs could take us, grateful for the guidance from our spirit friends. I carefully placed Ariana beside the grandfather rock. I said my prayers and asked for a healing blessing for Ariana. I cried out, "Please God, help her, help us. She's been a neglected child, and it has turned her into an evil witch. I know the most powerful weapon in the universe is love. And I know in my heart —because she was deprived of her mother at such a young age and wasn't given the love and support she needed, Ariana became evil. In some twisted way she thought that finding the Testament and the Seal would somehow bring her closer to her mom. Carole and I stand by her here today, asking You for help. We will come daily to the grandfather rock, until she is well. Please help to heal her darkened heart. Save her from her shadow self. Allow her to reach inside her mind to her most cherished moments with her mother. Let her remember the love her mother had for her when she was young. Please!" I beseeched.

Carole and I nodded at one another, and I appreciated her support and spiritual guidance. I felt our energies merge and placed my left hand on the grandfather rock and held Ariana's hand with my right. After a few minutes, Ariana awoke coughing and choking. We helped her sit up.

"Paige, what happened? What ... what am I doing here?" Ariana sputtered. "I had a visit from my mother. She's beautiful. I'd forgotten her somehow. Oh, my heart. It hurts so bad. It's aching. Help me! It's overpowering." And on that last woeful plea, Ariana fainted.

"Oh no! What have I done? Have I helped her or hurt her? Please tell me!" I cried out to our spirit friends.

Wait, my child; you shall see. The pureness in your heart, and Carole's, and the energy from the grandfather rock has healed her. Patience, Paige.

Carole and I both crashed next to Ariana. When we awoke, Ariana towered over us, smiling. "So nice to see you, Paige." And this time, it wasn't the voice of a dark spirit. "Oh, Paige, how can I ever thank you? I felt like I was wandering the grounds of hell, under a spell, and everything was mixed up. I sort of remember I tried to harm you, Carole. And Trixie and Allan. But most of all you, Paige. I'm so sorry. My heart had turned dark. It was black. It was horrible living like that. Hatred overcame my reasoning. How could I ever want to be on the demons' side? I'll spend eternity trying to get the stench from Beelzebul off me. And I never saw anything good in another human being or spirit. It was debilitating. Can you ever forgive me?"

I paused as she asked the final question. Then slowly, I replied, "I think the one you need forgiveness from is God. Of course I forgive you, my friend. I knew you were in there somewhere ... the good Ariana. Whenever someone said you were evil, I couldn't shake the feeling that the goodness within you had been taken hostage by your shadow self. We all have one, Ariana, our dark side. We have to embrace and understand this side of our soul in order to move past it and forward into the light. You have overcome, Ariana. Be proud of yourself. Carole and I were happy to help you find your way back. As much as you feel we helped you, you helped yourself. Your soul wanted to come into the light."

"Uh, Paige? Chill a minute," said Carole as she placed her hand on my arm. "Are you sure you're on the good side of things now, Ariana?"

"Yes, I feel like I'm wrapped in a warm, sunshine-filled hug full of love."

And for the first time in a long time, I saw Ariana smile. It was brilliant and beautiful. Her face flushed with colour instead of being pale as it had been before; now, it was all aglow. Even her straggly black hair was shiny and neat. Her eyes reflected light.

My dream had finally come true. In my heart of hearts, I always knew Ariana had a good side, a light side. Sometimes a friend needs to be shown love, understanding, and forgiveness before they can tap into it. I could only imagine how Ariana felt when, mistreated, neglected, and unwanted as a child ... the darkness set in and her shadow self took over. It was her defence mechanism. But it's within all of us to fight against our darker side, our shadow selves. And on that thought, a sudden, bright, white light appeared over Ariana's right shoulder and formed into what I hoped to be her mother.

"My daughter. You had become so lost. I tried to reach you so many times but you wouldn't let me in. You didn't sense my energy and therefore could not listen for my voice. It was heartbreaking to witness your actions. I'm so sorry I couldn't be there for you."

We watched as she hovered above us with her beautiful, strawberry blonde curly hair cascading down onto her full length white robe highlighting her green eyes; her face was filled with freckles like her daughter's.

"Thank you, Paige, for taking a leap of faith and helping to heal my daughter after all she did to you." She turned to Carole and said, "Bless you too, child. Thank you." Then, she gazed adoringly at Ariana. "I will watch over you, my daughter, until we meet again. Remember, I love you. Always." Ariana's mom faded away.

"Mom! Wait!" Ariana slumped to the ground and rolled onto her side, crying as she released her blackened, negative energy once and for all.

"Ariana, please know you will be reunited with your mother one day. It's not your time yet," Carole said. Her eyes brimmed with tears and empathy for our newfound friend.

I added, "You two have so much in common. And we're lucky, we all have each other." We were emotionally bonded, the three of us now fast friends. Finally, Ariana bolted upright and faced us.

"Live from a place of love; it conquers all that is evil." Ariana smiled and touched her heart. "I heard it over and over again and tried to ignore it. Now I understand it all, Paige. Thank you."

"Bingo! That's the answer," I cried. "You are healed, Ariana. Come. Carole, we must tell your dad and everyone."

The three of us raced off together through fields of lavender, laughing as we went.

EPILOGUE

"Do you know what you've done, Paige? You've cast the biggest threat to humankind, Beelzebul, into his fiery hell where he'll be trapped forever. Our Heavenly Father has seen to that. You have set humanity free to evolve, to cast away all fears, hatred, jealousies, insecurities, and greed. Without the control of Beelzebul and his influencers, humans can move on together with love in their hearts. They can learn to love each other as one and help each other, not wage wars, or worse. They can develop their intuitive gifts without fear or threat of evil possessing them. Well done, Paige." Archangel Michael gracefully collapsed his wings and patted me on the back. Then he smiled at me and continued.

"No one, other than your friends, will ever know the ordeal you've overcome here today. You are the Chosen One, Paige, a true soldier. We thank you for your perseverance and, most of all, for your love for humankind. You put yourself in harm's way and sacrificed for the greater good. You are pure of heart. You'll have your life back now. But we promise you, if evil finds its way back to you, we will protect you."

"Your soul rose up and cast the spell," Gabriel added, "the only spell that could send Beelzebul to his fiery prison. Your soul recited the Hebrew spell from the *Testament of Solomon* in Solomon's own words. It is not for any human to hear or speak. Only from your soul could you invoke this incantation. It was God's will."

An energy emanated from my body as he spoke, enveloping me in a cloak of warmth and protection.

Suddenly, Archangel Raphael spoke. "There she is. We can see your soul, Paige. You have mastered the ability to connect to your inner being. You are on a spiritual path that will last many more lifetimes. The healer in me will make sure to protect your health along the way."

I smiled and bowed my head, acknowledging the sanctity I was afforded by three commanding, spiritual enforcers of God's word, His highest angels. "Semper fidelis! Whenever you need me, I am here," I cried.

The Archangels Michael and Raphael stood side by each with their swords raised. Gabriel held up his right hand, and the three angels ascended to join their forces in Heaven. As I watched my friends, my protectors, soar to the upperworld, they were followed by a bright, white light. Its brilliance blinded me for a minute, and I closed my eyes, whispering a prayer of thanks and gratitude for their love and support. I opened my eyes to find an artistic masterpiece painted across the sky: the sun, crowned by a dazzling rainbow-coloured halo, floating high in the baby-blue sky, and the faces of my Heroes drawn into the clouds. A picture-perfect ending to a long, exhausting, but epoch-making day. At last I knew in my heart; love is, indeed, the most powerful weapon on Earth when paired with faith.

THE END

ACKNOWLEDGEMENTS

With deep gratitude, and a heartfelt thank you, to our son, J.R., for his inspiration, love, support, and exceptional writing skill. You have made your mom's dream come true. I am honoured to be your Mom, J.R., and your coauthor. I am forever grateful. Your Dad and I are so very proud of you.

Thank you ever so much to my soulmate and kind, loving husband, Kevin. Without your constant encouragement, this journey of mine would not have been given life. Paige's story may have been tucked in a drawer, forever, lost in a sea of papers. I am honoured to be your loving wife.

J.R. and I would like to thank my sisters, his aunts. Lynn is our number one supporter at our book signings and past editor of our first two novels. Thank you for sharing your expertise, Lynn, and your kind generosity of heart. Lynn passed the torch to our editor, Susan Hughes, My Independent Editor. I have enjoyed our conversations throughout the editing process, Susan. Thank you for your wisdom to both ladies. Thank you sister Cindy for creating the two new sketches of the O'Brien Estate and surrounding area. Without them, the Paige Maddison Series would be incomplete. Thank you for shining your light and letting your artistic ability flow. Very generous, indeed.

Thank you kindly to our niece/cousin, beta reader, Katy. You certainly 'shine your light'. Thank you for your heartfelt review of Book Three. To all of our nieces and nephews, J.R.'s cousins, we are so blessed to have you in our lives. We love each and every one of you. Thank you for your love and support.

A huge thank you to Ruth and John Robert Colombo for your wisdom, coaching, and hours of entertaining tales. Without the two of you, I would not have found the courage to stand up and speak my voice. Thank you so much, JR, for each and every blurb you've written for the Paige Maddison Series. We're forever grateful.

Thank you Karen for your ongoing cheerleading and being my lifelong best friend. Our discussions are priceless.

Thank you to my friend, Philip Henry, who is always ready to read the raw manuscript and help with the edits, and to provide a blurb. You truly are remarkable, my friend.

Thank you to David D. Plain for suggesting the Ojibwa chant included in *Shine Your Light*. And thank you for your kind blurb and generous support. We are forever thankful.

We cannot forget the musicians of the world! From Tony Orlando & Dawn, to Annie Lennox, Michael Jackson, Michelle Qureshi, and so many, many more. Our world would not be the same without the gift of music. We thank you kindly.

Until we meet again, don't forget to *Shine Your Light*.

Follow us on Facebook: www.facebook.com/leebicematheson

How about on Twitter: @BiceMatheson @justinrmatheson

Our website is: www.leebicematheson.ca

J.R. and I would love to hear your thoughts about *Shine Your Light*. If you enjoyed Paige's journey, won't you please write a review and post it on Goodreads, Amazon, Google Books, Apple iBooks, or your favourite site? It would mean the world to us. Thank you kindly for your generosity. Paige thanks you too ☺

For booking interviews, or media, please
email: info@leebicematheson.ca

ABOUT THE AUTHORS

Lee Bice-Matheson began her writing career as a storyteller, often weaving tales for her son, J.R. Matheson. Her stories parlayed into a writing career that was united with her son's creative imagination, as a mom-son writing team. It was her dream come true! Lee is proud to say they have coauthored Destiny's Gate, Book Two, and Shine Your Light, Book Three. Lee is also the author of Wake Me Up Inside, Book One, in the Paige Maddison Series. It was the recipient of the Literacy Award from the Readers' Advisory Panel, Orillia Public Library, and the Paige Maddison Series continues to be included in the Battle of the Books, Simcoe County. Lee is passionate about spirituality, and all it encompasses. She loves spending time in nature, especially canoeing and portaging into Algonquin Park with her husband. Lee has degrees in Honours History, Master of Library & Information Science, both from Western University. She has worked in public, medical, and corporate libraries, and now works proudly with her husband, Kevin, in their Chiropractic Clinic.

J.R. Matheson has been writing fantasy and horror since he was old enough to hold a pen. Collaborating on the Paige Maddison Series has reignited his passion for creative writing. When he's not weaving tales with his mom and coauthor, Lee Bice-Matheson, he can be found drowning in scientific publications and talking incessantly about his research at the Centre for Addiction and Mental Health (CAMH) in Toronto, Ontario, where he is a pharmacology PhD student. Some may claim that science and the creative arts are at odds, but J.R. feels they are one and the same.

Printed in Canada